The HOMEWORK MACHINE

The HOMEWORK MACHINE

AUTHOR OF NIGHTMARE AT THE BOOK FAIR

DAN GUTMAN

SIMON & SCHUSTER BOOKS FOR YOUNG READERS
New York   London   Toronto   Sydney

SIMON & SCHUSTER BOOKS FOR YOUNG READERS
An imprint of Simon & Schuster Children's Publishing Division
1230 Avenue of the Americas, New York, NY 10020
This book is a work of fiction. Any references to historical events, real people, or real locales are used fictitiously. Other names, characters, places, and incidents are the product of the author's imagination, and any resemblance to actual events or locales or persons, living or dead, is entirely coincidental.
Copyright © 2006 by Dan Gutman

SIMON & SCHUSTER BOOKS FOR YOUNG READERS is a trademark of Simon & Schuster, Inc.
For information about special discounts for bulk purchases, please contact Simon & Schuster Special Sales at 1-866-506-1949 or business@simonandschuster.com.
The Simon & Schuster Speakers Bureau can bring authors to your live event. For more information or to book an event, contact the Simon & Schuster Speakers Bureau at 1-866-248-3049 or visit our website at www.simonspeakers.com.
Also available in a Simon and Schuster Books for Young Readers hardcover edition.
Designed by Christopher Grassi
The text of this book was set in Horley Old Style.
Manufactured in the United States of America • 1010 OFF
First paperback edition June 2007
18 20 19 17
The Library of Congress has cataloged the hardcover edition as follows:
Gutman, Dan.
The homework machine / by Dan Gutman.—1st ed.
p. cm.
Summary: Four fifth-grade students—a geek, a class clown, a teacher's pet, and a slacker—as well as their teachers and mothers, each relate events surrounding a computer programmed to complete homework assignments.
[1.Homework—Fiction. 2. Cheating—Fiction. 3. Schools—Fiction. 4. Interpersonal relations—Fiction. 5. Arizona—Fiction.] I. Title.
PZ7.G9846Hnw 2006
[Fic]—dc22
2005019785
ISBN: 978-0-689-87678-3 (hc)
ISBN: 978-0-689-87679-0 (pbk)
ISBN: 978-1-4424-0709-1 (eBook)

To kids who hate homework . . .
but do it anyway

Introduction

POLICE CHIEF REBECCA FISH, GRAND CANYON, ARIZONA

Seen a lot of strange stuff go down in ten years working here. Probably has something to do with being so close to the canyon. Having a mile-deep hole in your backyard brings out the weirdness in folks.

I remember the time that gambler from L.A. lost a bet in Las Vegas, and his friends drove him up here. Forced him to parachute into the canyon. Guy almost died. You get all kinds in this part of the country. The canyon attracts 'em like flies to dog doo. But this recent situation involving the children was one of the stranger cases I ever ran into.

We called in everybody who had anything to do with what happened and taped their private testimony for the record. Far as I'm concerned, this case is closed and shut. Let's hope these four students learned their lesson. This'll never happen again, that's for darn sure.

Chapter 1

September

SAM DAWKINS. GRADE 5

The police lady says me and Brenton and Judy and Kelsey have to each come in separately and talk about what happened.

Okay, so here goes. Is this thing on? My name is Sam Dawkins, but everybody calls me Snikwad on account of that's my last name spelled backward. *Dawkins. Snikwad.* Get it? Most kids call me "Snik." It's kinda cool. Beats having a nickname like Booger Face or Fart Boy or something stupid like that.

I was new to the school. I didn't know anything. And I *didn't* get kicked out of my old school because I refused to get a haircut. That's a lie. I don't know how that rumor got started. I don't care if you believe me. That's the truth.

3

Anyway, my parents moved here from Oregon. My dad was in the air force and that's why we moved to Arizona. He was assigned to Luke Air Force Base near Phoenix.

The bottom line is, we messed up. Stuff happens. We're not perfect. We all feel bad. We won't do it again. What are you gonna do, throw us in jail? That's my statement.

What, you need more than that? Details? Okay, okay. What do you want to know?

KELSEY DONNELLY, GRADE 5

My name is Kelsey Donnelly. I really don't see the reason why we gotta do this. The police lady told me that I have to make a "statement" in private and tell the whole story of what happened from the very beginning in September. Like I'm a creep or something! I barely remember what happened last week. Forget about way back in September.

Look, we're sorry about what happened. We were just having a little fun and it got out of hand. It's not like we robbed a bank or anything. That's my statement. I can't believe I have to spend my summer in this room with a tape recorder when I could be out having fun. Can I go now?

JUDY DOUGLAS. GRADE 5

My name is Judy Douglas. My mom works at home and my dad works for the National Park Service. He cuts down dead trees and does controlled burns to prevent forest fires.

The whole thing started because certain people who shall remain nameless did some thoughtless things that I don't need to discuss here.

This is so unfair. I have almost straight A's and I'm in the G&T program. That's gifted and talented. I would never break the law or do anything dishonest. Things just got out of control. The next thing we knew, we had to go talk to the police.

Do you have any idea of how humiliating this entire ordeal has been for me? Do you know how upset my parents were when they found out? And now this is going to be on my permanent record, probably for the rest of my life. If this keeps me out of law school someday, I will be so angry.

I'll sue. That's what I'll do. Well, if I get into law school I'll sue. But if I get into law school I won't need to sue. Oh, I just wish I could go to sleep and wake up and find out it was all a dream. Like it never happened.

JUDY'S MOM

My first reaction was that it was discrimination. We are one of the few African-American families living in this area. When something bad happens to Judy, I can't help but wonder if it is bigotry at work. But I looked into it, and that wasn't the case. She and the others just did a dumb thing and they got caught. It's as simple as that. And now they're going to have to pay for it.

BRENTON DAMAGATCHI, GRADE 5

It's interesting how things happen sometimes. If I line up ten dominoes and I push over the first one, the others will fall one by one. But if I leave the first one alone, the other dominoes remain standing.

Life is like that. The way your life plays out depends on which dominoes you choose to push over and which ones you leave alone. In this case, we pushed over the wrong domino. Can I get a drink of water or something?

MISS RASMUSSEN, FIFTH-GRADE TEACHER

I was so excited, walking into my very own classroom for the first time in September. I had been a student teacher in Ohio, and I was hoping to get a job somewhere in the west, preferably near a national park. I've always been a nature lover, and I wanted to share this with young people. When I got an offer to teach fifth grade at the Grand Canyon School, well, it was one of the best things that ever happened to me.

The Grand Canyon! I had never even been here before. Just think! Over the course of four billion years, the Colorado River slowly sliced this gash into the Earth. I spent hours exploring it when I moved here, and took lots of pictures of the layers of rock. The Grand Canyon is like a sculpture, created by nature. I was in awe.

JUDY DOUGLAS, GRADE 5

When I walked into Miss Rasmussen's class on the first day of school, the first thing that struck me was that she was so *young*! I mean, she looked like she could have been one of the students. I liked that, because I figured she would be really enthusiastic about everything. Some of the older teachers who have been teaching all their lives don't get too excited about anything anymore.

On the other hand, I was afraid Miss Rasmussen might not be experienced enough to handle some of the boys, who can be a problem sometimes.

SAM DAWKINS. GRADE 5

So I walk into Miss Rasmussen's class on the first day of school in September and I'm the new kid, so I'm a little nervous and I don't want everybody looking at me, but they're all looking at me anyway because, well, I'm the new kid and everybody wants to check out the new kid.

I scope out the scene and it's obvious who the cool kids are, who the dumb kids are, who the smart kids are, and who the dorks are. I could tell in a minute. The class had the usual number of clueless dweebs, pre–jock idiots, losers, brown-nosers, and bullies, just like my old school.

But the one kid who stood out was Brenton. You just knew the first time you set eyes on him that there was something different about this kid.

JUDY DOUGLAS. GRADE 5

Brenton would dress funny, with these stiff long pants no matter how hot it was. He always wore a button-down shirt and sometimes he would even wear a tie to school. Can you imagine? I guess his mom made him dress that way. I hope so, anyway. I can't imagine a boy wearing a tie to school on his own. He was actually pretty good-looking, but he combed his hair in a really weird way. Like he parted it on the wrong side or something.

Once I suggested to him that he would look better if he combed his hair the other way. He just looked at me like I was crazy. Like it hadn't even occurred to him that you could change your personal appearance to look better. Or that it would matter. He probably had so many more important things on his mind that he couldn't be bothered with something as trivial as combing his hair.

Some of the other kids would make fun of him behind his back. Sometimes in *front* of his back. He didn't have any friends. Nobody seemed to know what to make of him.

SAM DAWKINS, GRADE 5

Brenton just came out and said the weirdest stuff. Like one time he comes up to me and asks me if I know what they made glass out of. I say no and he says they make glass out of sand. I say that's interesting, even though I really don't think it's all that interesting. Then he gets that look in his eyes and he says they take *sand* and make it into *glass*. He says he figures that if they can turn sand into glass, just about anything is possible. I'm telling you, the guy is different.

KELSEY DONNELLY, GRADE 5

Brenton was a genius when it came to school and stuff, but he was real stupid when it came to other stuff. I remember one time this reality TV show was hot and everybody was talking about it. I mean *everybody*. And we were all at recess talking about it and Brenton comes out and says something like, "I never heard of that show." We all just looked at him. It was like not knowing the sun was in the sky. And they say I'm dumb!

That's just the way Brenton is. He doesn't know or care about the stuff that normal people care about. We all thought he was a dork. Well, probably Judy didn't, 'cause she's a genius too.

SAM DAWKINS, GRADE 5

Most kids at least *try* to act cool in some way. You know, like they'll get T-shirts with cool logos on them or they'll get a cool bike or listen to cool music. They may not be cool themselves, but they make themselves cool by having cool stuff or hanging around with cool people. But Brenton, he didn't even make the effort.

BRENTON DAMAGATCHI, GRADE 5

What does "cool" mean, anyway? Did you know that Abraham Lincoln once said "That is cool"? It's true. I looked it up. He said it in his famous Cooper Union speech. Google it if you don't believe me.

I feel that a person can change himself or herself no more than a giraffe can decide it doesn't like having a long neck. It would be easy enough to buy the latest clothes and watch the hot new TV shows and surround myself with cool things. But that wouldn't make me cool. Nothing will ever make me cool. Some people are simply destined not to be cool. And I'm cool with that.

If everybody was cool, everybody would be the same. Nobody would be cooler than anyone else. There would be nobody to make fun of. So I suppose I serve a purpose, in a weird way.

MISS RASMUSSEN, FIFTH-GRADE TEACHER

Our claim to fame at the Grand Canyon School is that we are the closest school to the Grand Canyon. We're about a half a mile from the South Rim. If you've ever been to the canyon, our school is south of El Tovar and near Bright Angel.

We go all the way from kindergarten to twelfth grade, and I believe we have the only high school that is in a national park.

By September, most of the tourists have gone back to work and school. It gets pretty quiet around here. But it's nice in a way, because we have the canyon to ourselves. We've got a lot of great teachers, nice parents, and good kids here. But sometimes, I guess, good kids do bad things.

SAM DAWKINS. GRADE 5

Somebody told me that the human brain isn't fully formed until we're about twenty years old. That's why kids do dumb things sometimes. And that's why we're not allowed to vote and drink and stuff. So can you really blame us for the dumb thing we did? I don't think so. Our brains aren't fully formed yet.

MISS RASMUSSEN. FIFTH-GRADE TEACHER

Some teachers like to have the desks arranged in perfect columns and rows. In graduate school, one of my professors told me that the children learn better when they work in small groups. I divided the class into six groups of four kids, and we pushed the desks together in those groups.

I had no big plan to put Brenton, Kelsey, Judy, and Sam together. I did it alphabetically. All their last names started with D. We called them the D Squad.

Every child is unique, of course. It's necessary to treat them as individuals. Just like me, Sam was new to this area, and he had some initial problems adjusting to the curriculum and the other students. Judy seemed very studious from the start, and I could tell that it was very important for her to be a high achiever. Kelsey was the opposite. She didn't appear to like school very much. And Brenton, well, Brenton was . . . different.

BRENTON DAMAGATCHI, GRADE 5

It makes no difference to me where I sit. I'll get the same information whether I'm sitting on one side of the room or the other. I don't ordinarily strike up friendships with my classmates. Snik, Judy, and Kelsey pretty much ignored me, and I ignored them. At least in September. It was fine.

BRENTON'S MOM

He was always different, from the moment he was born. I don't think he ever cried when he was a baby. Not even once. When he was hungry, he would just look at me with this look that said, "If I could speak, I would be saying I need a bottle."

He spoke very early. He had no interest in watching television or playing with other children. Instead, he would play chess against himself. He taught himself how to play the piano as soon as he was big enough to climb up on the bench. When he was just six, he wrote a concerto. Really! And that's what he called it, too. "My concerto." I don't know where he got the word "concerto." I still don't know what it means. He was very special.

BRENTON DAMAGATCHI, GRADE 5

I was thinking of starting a club for kids like me, who don't particularly enjoy the company of other people. We could call it The Antisocial Club. We could hold meetings and talk about the best ways to avoid other people. But then I decided that the best way to avoid other people would be to not start the club.

KELSEY DONNELLY, GRADE 5

The good thing about sitting at Brenton's table was that you could copy answers off him. He knew everything, and he didn't care if you peeked at his papers. That's the only reason I got a B in math for the first marking period. I copied off Brenton.

SAM DAWKINS, GRADE 5

What did I think of the other kids at my table when I first met them? Let me think. First impressions? Judy: stuck-up. Kelsey: a loser. Brenton: mutant dork from another planet. I was the only cool one.

JUDY DOUGLAS, GRADE 5

Oh, I didn't like Snik at all in the beginning. He had really long hair, which I personally think looks terrible on a boy. And he had this very smart-alecky "I hate the world" attitude. It's typical of boys with low self-esteem, I understand. He struck me as, and I hate to say this, but he struck me as stupid.

Kelsey, well, she just didn't seem to care about anything, and I found it very hard to relate to her because I care so much about everything. She and Snik were not the kind of people I would ever hang around with.

Brenton . . . What can I say about him? I was

in awe of him. I've been in Brenton's class ever since first grade, and he was always smarter than me. I try so hard all the time and he never seemed like he was trying at all. I was in awe of his natural intelligence. I had never met anyone who was smarter than me. I almost felt like nobody should be allowed to be that brilliant. I never made fun of Brenton the way other kids did.

RONNIE TEOTWAWKI, GRADE 5

My name is Ronnie Teotwawki. I sat on the other side of the room, near the cloakroom. Why do I have to be here? I didn't have anything to do with it.

I never wanted to sit with any of those D Squad losers. Snikwad is a jerk. Everybody knows he got thrown out of his last school. Personally, I loved it when the four of them got in trouble. It took the attention off me.

KELSEY DONNELLY, GRADE 5

I guess it all started because of homework. Homework sucks, but I do it. It would suck even worse to fail and have to repeat a grade because I didn't do my homework.

SAM DAWKINS, GRADE 5

I've always been antihomework, and I'll tell you why. We work at school all day long. Then, finally, three o'clock comes and we can go home. And what do we have to do at home? More schoolwork! It's not fair. When I get home from school, my brain needs a rest. I want to hang out and watch some TV or play video games. Homework is like punishment you get just for being a kid.

MISS RASMUSSEN, FIFTH-GRADE TEACHER

I came across a worksheet titled "The Ten Commandments of Homework." I made a copy for everyone in the class. For their first homework assignment of the year, I asked everyone to write his or her feelings about it.

The Ten Commandments of Homework

1. Homework is an essential part of learning.
2. Not doing your homework because you do not believe in homework is self-defeating behavior.
3. Keep track of your daily assignments.
4. The more you review information, the easier it is to remember and the longer you are able to retain it. Even though you may not have written work to

17

do, you can always review or reread assignments.

5. It is your responsibility to find out what you have missed when you are absent. Take the initiative to ask a classmate or teacher what you need to make up.

6. Have a place to study that works for you, one that is free from distractions. Be honest with yourself about how well you study when the TV or stereo is playing.

7. Make sure you have everything you need before you begin to work.

8. Develop a schedule you can follow.

9. Be rested when you study. It is okay to study in short blocks of time. Marathon study sessions may be self-defeating. Study for 30 to 40 minutes at a time, then take a 5- to 10-minute break. Estimate the amount of time it will take to do an assignment and plan your break time accordingly.

10. Prioritize your homework so that you begin with the most important assignment first. For instance, study for a test and then do the daily assignment.

SAM DAWKINS. GRADE 5

Miss R. gave us this dumb assignment to write about those Ten Commandments of Homework. This is what I turned in:

Snikwad's Ten Commandments of Homework

1. We live in a democracy, where we have freedom, right? We're entitled to life, liberty, and the pursuit of happiness. So how can I pursue happiness if I have to spend every night doing homework? Homework is cruel, totalitarian punishment created by grown-ups to take away the freedoms of poor, defenseless children.

2. Nobody ever saved a life, won a war, stopped a crime, or cured a disease while they were doing homework. Think of all the good things we could be accomplishing if we didn't have to spend so much time doing homework.

3. Doing homework causes eyestrain, fatigue, insomnia, and other physical ailments.

4. Thomas Edison went to school for four months. He never did any homework, and look how he turned out.

5. There's a name for working without getting paid. It's called slavery, and it was banned during the Civil War. If kids are forced to do homework, they should be paid for it.

6. Homework is proof of teacher incompetence. If a teacher is any good, students would learn the stuff in school and wouldn't have to learn it again at home.

7. Doing homework wastes valuable natural resources.

We have to use lots of energy to keep all those lightbulbs burning. We have to cut down trees to make paper and pencils. We'd save a lot of energy by banning homework.

8. I keep hearing that American kids are way too fat, and that's because we don't get enough exercise. For every minute kids are doing homework, we are getting fatter. Kids should be outside running around and getting exercise, not inside doing worksheets.

9. Virtually every known murderer, bank robber, and criminal did homework when they were children. How can we be sure the homework didn't cause the criminal behavior?

10. Homework sucks. There should be a constitutional amendment banning it.

MISS RASMUSSEN, FIFTH-GRADE TEACHER

I didn't like what Sam wrote, but I gave him a B for using his creativity.

SAM'S MOM

We've had to move around a lot, and Sam never got to stay in one school very long. My husband was stationed in Oregon and we liked living there. But Sam was going through a difficult phase and he got suspended from school last year. We thought it would be a good idea to move and get a fresh start somewhere else. There's an air force base near Phoenix. My husband requested a transfer, and that's what brought us here. That was before the war broke out, of course.

Back in Oregon, Sam simply refused to get a haircut, and he refused to do his homework. We couldn't do anything to help him. What are you supposed to do, strap your child to a chair and whip him? Kids reach an age when they naturally become defiant.

So we made a deal with Sam. He didn't have to get a haircut if he would do his homework. We figured that homework was more important than hair. When it comes to raising kids, you have to choose your battles. His hair looked horrible, but at least he was doing his homework.

JUDY DOUGLAS, GRADE 5

Okay, I admit it. I *like* homework. Kids make fun of me and all, but I think it's necessary and a part of our education. Homework reinforces what we learn in school each day. My friends and I used to go over each other's houses and do our homework together. It was fun. It was a social thing. I always thought Snik made a big deal out of nothing. It's just homework.

MISS RASMUSSEN, FIFTH-GRADE TEACHER

Compared to other teachers, I don't even really assign that much homework. I give the students about forty-five minutes a night. That's it. It was a lot different when I was a child. I remember spending hours every night doing homework. I practically lived in the library. I never complained. Back in those days, if you didn't do your homework or you misbehaved, you might get a yardstick rapped against your knuckles. Today, of course, we don't do that. Then again, I'd say the kids aren't as motivated these days, either.

We study a lot about Arizona history and geography of the western United States in fifth grade, so we devote a lot of time to that. We also cover the solar system. Explorers. Things like that. I thought the kids would like it. The homework isn't hard.

SAM DAWKINS, GRADE 5

So one day back in September, Miss Rasmussen passes out our homework assignment just as the bell rings. I'm in a bad mood because it's been a long day and I just don't feel like going home to do more schoolwork. You know what I mean. And I look over at Brenton. He sticks the homework assignment in his backpack like it doesn't bother him at all. You could give him *ten* hours of homework and he'd be perfectly happy. The kid is like a human computer.

So I start in on him, saying he probably spends all his free time doing homework. And he says something in that voice of his like, "Well, no, actually I don't spend *any* time at all doing homework."

Say what? I ask him if he's got a brother or sister who does his homework for him. That would be a sweet deal, right? He says no. He says he invented a machine that does his homework for him. I said, "Get outta town!"

That's the first I heard of the homework machine.

BRENTON DAMAGATCHI, GRADE 5

It was a mistake on my part. I allowed my emotions to govern my behavior. But I have never understood why average and under-average students feel a necessity to poke fun at those of us who work hard and do well in school. If anything, it should be the other way around. I suppose I didn't appreciate Snik making fun of me. But it was a fatal blunder on my part to have told him about the homework machine. I accept full responsibility.

Chapter 2

October

JUDY DOUGLAS, GRADE 5

I remember that day we first heard about the homework machine. It was late September, maybe early October. I heard Brenton and Snik talking. Or at least I heard Brenton say something about a machine that does your homework for you. A homework machine? Can you imagine? It sounded like science fiction. It sounded like a joke.

But Brenton isn't exactly known for his sense of humor. In fact, I don't think I've ever heard him crack a joke. At least not on purpose. Sometimes the kids laugh at the things he says when he's trying to be serious. Not me. That's rude.

I thought about raising my hand and telling

Miss Rasmussen what I had overheard. But I knew everybody already thought I was a big Goody Two-shoes and I didn't want them calling me a tattletale too. Maybe I *should* have told Miss Rasmussen. None of this would have happened. I might have mentioned it to Kelsey.

KELSEY DONNELLY, GRADE 5

Oh, I totally believed it. Brenton's a dork, but he's a genius dork. I know he's gonna find a cure for cancer or win the Nobel prize or something when he grows up. If any kid could create a machine that would do your homework for you, Brenton is the kid.

And what's so amazing about it, anyhow? They put a man on the moon, right? They grow babies in test tubes, right? So why couldn't somebody invent a machine that could do homework?

BRENTON DAMAGATCHI, GRADE 5

I knew I should never have told Snik. As soon as the words left my mouth, I realized it was a mistake. Secrets are best kept secret. That's why they're called secrets. If I had kept my mouth shut, none of this would have happened.

SAM DAWKINS, GRADE 5

I say to Brenton, "Get outta town! There's no such thing as a machine that can do your homework for you." He says there is too, and he's got one. I tell him that if he really has a machine like that, he should show it to me. Put up or shut up, right? And when he says he doesn't want to, I just say that's proof that he made the whole thing up. He looks all guilty, like maybe he's gonna cry or something.

JUDY DOUGLAS, GRADE 5

I told Snik to leave Brenton alone. But he wouldn't. He pestered him all the way out to the playground. It was really mean. Snik is one of those kids who doesn't know when to stop. He'll do something mean or say something mean and you tell him to stop it, but he'll keep doing it. Then you raise your voice a little and say stop it and he keeps doing it. And then, finally, you shout at him, "STOP IT!" and he acts like, "Whoa! You don't have to SHOUT!" But you *do* have to shout. Because if you don't shout, he doesn't get the message. And Brenton never shouts.

BRENTON DAMAGATCHI, GRADE 5

I didn't want to show the machine to anyone. I never planned to show it to anyone. But Snik was really giving me a hard time. He called me a liar and a fake, which I am not.

KELSEY DONNELLY, GRADE 5

I thought Brenton was gonna cry, really. Judy and me told Snik to knock it off.

BRENTON DAMAGATCHI, GRADE 5

Finally I said to them, "Fine, come over to my house after school today and I'll show it to you. But you have to swear on your life you'll never tell anybody about it."

JUDY DOUGLAS, GRADE 5

If he really *did* have a machine that could do your homework for you, I wanted to see it. I work so hard on my homework and Brenton still gets better grades than I do. I wanted to see what tricks he was using.

KELSEY DONNELLY, GRADE 5

I didn't even want to go to Brenton's house. But I had nothing else going on after school, so I figured what the heck. Beats sitting around. We rode our bikes over.

BRENTON'S MOM

You can imagine my surprise when Brenton came home from school with that boy Sam who they call Snikwad and these two girls. I don't remember the last time Brenton had a friend over. Maybe when he was a toddler and the kids had what we used to call "play dates." And he *never* had a girl over.

When he was little, the other kids never seemed to like him, or they couldn't relate to him. I really didn't know what was going on. It was always a matter of concern. I hoped he would grow out of it as he got older, and he would eventually fit in better socially.

I was thrilled when the three of them came over. I thought that maybe Brenton had finally made some friends at school. I quickly whipped up a batch of those cinnamon rolls from a can and brought them up to his room for the kids. Just trying to be hospitable, you know?

I wanted to hang around and get to know them a little, but they acted like they wanted me out of the room. So I went back downstairs. After all that happened later, I wish I had stayed.

JUDY DOUGLAS, GRADE 5

I always wondered what Brenton's house would look like, what his mom would be like. Well, it was lovely and so was she. She even made us these delicious cinnamon rolls.

SAM DAWKINS, GRADE 5

Brenton's room is weird. Most guys put up posters on their walls with pictures of their favorite athletes or rock bands or dirt bikes and stuff like that. Brenton has a picture of some old dude from ancient history.

I say who's that and he says it's Leonardo DaVinci and I say isn't he the dude who was in that *Titanic* movie and he says no he's the dude who painted the Mona Lisa and I say the Mona what and he says oh forget about it. Have another cinnamon roll. So I did.

He has some bumper sticker on the back of his door that says "War is not the answer" or something like that. That got me. You know, my dad was in the military and these people who don't support the military get me really angry. I told him he was a hippie and a commie and stuff like that, joking around, but not really.

BRENTON DAMAGATCHI. GRADE 5

I explained to Sam it is possible to support the military and at the same time be against the war. To me, the best support you can give to the military is to keep them out of wars unless it's in our nation's vital interest. He didn't understand. I didn't press it. These issues tend to make people very emotional and are best avoided.

JUDY DOUGLAS. GRADE 5

Brenton closed the door as soon as his mom left. He locked it, too. I was looking around the room for a machine, but Brenton just sat down in front of the computer on his desk. It was nice, but it didn't look like anything special. I mean, just about everybody has a computer. There was a scanner and a printer attached to it, but that was about it. Brenton said his dad works for a computer company, so he gets all kinds of stuff for free.

KELSEY DONNELLY. GRADE 5

Brenton said so you want to see how the homework machine works? We all said yeah. He took a piece of blank paper and wrote this on it:

$2 + 2 =$

Then he put the paper into the scanner,

facedown. He sat at the keyboard and typed some stuff into it. A few seconds later, the printer started making noise and a piece of paper popped out of it. The paper said on it:

$2 + 2 = 4$

SAM DAWKINS, GRADE 5

I say that's *it*? *That's* the famous homework machine you told us about? Big deal! I just laughed my head off. Any kid in first grade can tell you that two plus two equals four. I've got a cheap calculator that can do a lot more than that. The whole thing looked bogus to me. What a joke! I couldn't believe he called that piece of junk a homework machine.

BRENTON'S MOM

I sat downstairs the whole time wondering what they were doing up there. I thought about going upstairs and putting my ear to the door to listen, but that would have been an invasion of their privacy. Plus, they might have opened the door and caught me.

JUDY DOUGLAS, GRADE 5

I felt sorry for Brenton. I figured he made up the story about the homework machine so he would make some friends. He probably just wanted us to come over to his house. It was kind of sad, really. I told Brenton I thought his machine was cool, because I didn't want to hurt his feelings.

BRENTON DAMAGATCHI. GRADE 5

They didn't quite grasp the concept at first. I just did the simple arithmetic problem as an example. If the machine could add two plus two, it could add *any* numbers. More than that, it could seek out *any* information on any subject.

They lacked vision. They could only see the paper in front of them.

SAM DAWKINS. GRADE 5

So Brenton grabs his backpack and pulls out the homework assignment for that night. It was all this stuff about the solar system.

Miss Rasmussen   Science homework

Name: _____

Instructions: Fill in the blanks.

Our Solar System

1. The Earth is _____ miles from the sun.

2. The closest planet to the sun is _____.

3. The word "galaxy" comes from the Greek word for _____.

4. The sun rises in the _____ and sets in the _____.

5. Groups of stars are called _____.

6. The Earth makes _____ revolution(s) around the sun each year.

7. When the moon is between the Earth and the sun, it is called a _____ moo

8. A rock or metal fragment in space is called a _____.

9. A chunk that lands on Earth is called a _____.

10. Mercury and Venus have _____ moons.

11. Earth's _____ hemisphere is tipped toward the sun in July.

12. Pluto was discovered in 1930 by _____ _____.

13. Haley's comet visits Earth every _____ years.

14. The diameter of the Earth at the equator is _____ miles.

15. Right now, the Earth is moving at a speed of _____ miles per second.

MISS RASMUSSEN, FIFTH-GRADE TEACHER

I don't believe in tests for fifth graders. At this age, I would rather the kids not feel so much pressure. Their daily homework assignments and special projects are more important and more educational. I usually give assignments in which the students have to answer multiple-choice questions or provide short answers. They're easier to grade.

KELSEY DONNELLY, GRADE 5

Brenton slipped the sheet into the scanner and sat down at the computer again. We were all making faces behind his back and rolling our eyes and trying not to laugh. He typed in a bunch of stuff just like before.

JUDY DOUGLAS, GRADE 5

Nothing happened for a long time. Like, over a minute. It was really awkward. We all sat there without making a sound. Brenton kept saying it will only take a minute or so and just be patient. The computer made some noises, but nothing seemed to be happening.

I think I was the one who said that I really should be getting home. I was embarrassed for

Brenton. I didn't want to see him fail, and I didn't want Snik to humiliate him.

SAM DAWKINS, GRADE 5

I'm sitting there the whole time thinking how much fun it's gonna be to tell everybody at school about Brenton's totally lame homework machine. But then the printer starts making that humming sound.

KELSEY DONNELLY, GRADE 5

The printer made some noise and Brenton sat back in his chair.

JUDY DOUGLAS, GRADE 5

The paper slid out of the printer. I was sitting on that side, so I picked it out.

Miss Rasmussen **Science homework**

Name: _Brenton Damagatchi_

Instructions: Fill in the blanks.

Our Solar System

1. The Earth is _93 mil._ miles from the sun.

2. The closest planet to the sun is _Mercury_.

3. The word "galaxy" comes from the Greek word for _milky way_.

4. The sun rises in the _east_ and sets in the _west_.

5. Groups of stars are called _galaxies_.

6. The Earth makes _1_ revolution(s) around the sun each year.

7. When the moon is between the Earth and the sun, it is called a _new_ moon.

8. A rock or metal fragment in space is called a _meteoroid_.

9. A chunk that lands on Earth is called a _meteorite_.

10. Mercury and Venus have _no_ moons.

11. Earth's _northern_ hemisphere is tipped toward the sun in July.

12. Pluto was discovered in 1930 by _Clyde_ _Tombaugh_.

13. Haley's comet visits Earth every _76_ years.

14. The diameter of the Earth at the equator is _7,926_ miles.

15. Right now, the Earth is moving at a speed of _18.5_ miles per second.

And for the longest time, we all just looked at it. I didn't know what to say. Nobody knew what to say.

SAM DAWKINS, GRADE 5

The thing *worked*! The thing freaking worked! Every question was answered. The answers were all right, it seemed to me. Not only that, but the answers were written in Brenton's handwriting. And the letters were even in blue ink. I mean, it was perfect! You'd never know that a machine did it. I couldn't believe my own eyes.

JUDY DOUGLAS, GRADE 5

We were all stunned. It was just amazing. It would have taken me a half an hour to look up all that information. Brenton just slipped the paper into the scanner and the answers popped out a minute later. If I hadn't seen it with my own eyes, I would never have believed it.

KELSEY DONNELLY, GRADE 5

I figured it was a trick. It had to be. Like there had to be a little man inside the computer who did the work. But there wasn't. It was an honest to goodness homework machine.

Of course it worked. I put the system together over the summer and started using it for my homework starting in September.

I really have nothing against doing homework, honestly. But it can be time-consuming. Having the machine do the homework for me allows me to pursue other interests. I want to find out more about psychology, physics, and medicine. I hope to find a cure for spinal-cord injuries someday.

There are only twenty-four hours in a day, unfortunately. The homework machine gave me more time. Sometimes I wish I lived on Venus or Mercury. Did you know that it takes 176 Earth days for Mercury to make one rotation, and it takes 243 Earth days for Venus to make one rotation? So a day on Venus lasts 243 Earth days. How much more could one accomplish in a lifetime if each day lasted that long?

On the other hand, it would suck to live on Jupiter. A day there lasts only ten hours. You couldn't get much done in that time at all. Plus, the planet is pretty much a giant ball of gas, which would be difficult to live on.

MISS RASMUSSEN. FIFTH-GRADE TEACHER

Sadly, Brenton is not challenged enough at our school. We simply don't have the resources to stimulate his mind properly. He needs to be in a school for special students like himself. He should be taking high school–level classes. I certainly enjoyed having him in my class, but sometimes I felt that he was bored there. I have to teach for *all* the kids.

In October, we did a special project in which I asked the students to design a catapult. You know, those machines they used in ancient times to hurl rocks and things? I thought this would be a good assignment because they would be learning about science, history, and physics, and they'd be having fun at the same time.

Well, all the kids came in with these adorable little catapults made out of Popsicle sticks and plastic spoons and rubber bands. Except for Brenton. His catapult was the size of a desk. It had ropes and springs and pulleys and levers. It even had a computer chip in it to help you aim the projectile you were firing. I didn't even understand it. It was simply amazing.

We took all the catapults out to the playground

and had a little contest. Most of them didn't work very well, but Brenton's threw a basketball over the school!

I was sure that Brenton's father must have done all the work. Parents do that sometimes, and I knew that Brenton's father was a very smart man who worked in the computer industry. But no, at our parent-teacher conference, Mr. Damagatchi told me he didn't even know Brenton had made a catapult. That was after Brenton brought it home and stored it in the garage.

BRENTON DAMAGATCHI, GRADE 5

You want to know about the catapult? I did a little research into Greek and Roman history. The basic principles of the catapult were known back in the ninth century B.C. I merely refined them. I don't want to bore you with all the details, but basically, all the parts of the catapult need to be proportional to the size of the torsion springs. It's simple mechanics, really. That kind of thing was fun for me. I never would have used the home-work machine for something like the catapult assignment.

SAM DAWKINS, GRADE 5

Catapults are cool. Miss R. showed us some Web site that said the Romans didn't have gunpowder back then, so they used catapults to fling boulders and burning garbage and even dead bodies at their enemies in a war. Can you imagine you're fighting somebody and they start heaving rotten food and stuff at you? War was cool even back then. That was the first time I ever had a homework assignment that was cool.

JUDY DOUGLAS, GRADE 5

I didn't like that catapult assignment at all. I didn't think that war was an appropriate subject for us to study in school. There are more important things for us to learn.

KELSEY DONNELLY, GRADE 5

My catapult sucked. It could barely throw a Ping-Pong ball ten feet. Everybody cracked up.

Where was I? Oh yeah, so the paper popped out of Brenton's printer and the worksheet was all filled out. After we realized the homework machine was for real, we were all talking at once, asking Brenton how it worked, how he invented it, how smart it was, and stuff like that.

BRENTON DAMAGATCHI, GRADE 5

The machine is simple, really. The scanner scans the worksheet and feeds the data into the computer. That's no big deal. I modified pattern-recognition software that would interpret the words and numbers, to figure out what is being asked.

If the information is already in the computer, such as the sum of two plus two, the computer simply spits out the answer and the printer prints out a duplicate copy of the worksheet with the answers. If the information is *not* in the computer, such as the diameter of the Earth, the computer automatically goes to the Internet, where virtually all of the world's knowledge is stored in digital form. It seeks out the answer from the most reliable Web site, cross-checks it against other Web sites, and the printer prints it out. The most difficult part was designing the software to print the answers in a typeface that looked like my own handwriting.

It's not science fiction. It's pretty basic stuff, really. I'm surprised nobody else thought of it before me.

SAM DAWKINS, GRADE 5

Once I see the thing in action, I go ballistic. I say to myself, this is better than Edison's invention of the lightbulb. This is better than the Wright brothers' invention of the airplane. This is the answer to all my prayers.

Homework was the one thing I hated more than anything else in the world. Homework was the thing that made life so difficult. If I play my cards right, I say to myself, I'll never have to do it again.

Suddenly I realized that for all his dorkiness, Brenton was the kind of kid I really want to hang out with.

JUDY DOUGLAS, GRADE 5

When that piece of paper popped out of the printer, I felt like I was witnessing a history-making event.

BRENTON DAMAGATCHI, GRADE 5

There was one thing I never told anyone. Shortly after I started using the homework machine for my own purposes, I received a mysterious e-mail. It was from somebody who said he'd like to meet me. That's all it said. At the bottom of the e-mail there was a name: R. Milner. I know better than to respond to strangers online. He could have been crazy, or a child molester, or whatever. I ignored the message.

KELSEY DONNELLY, GRADE 5

It was cool. Definitely cool. I couldn't wait until we got our next homework assignment so we could try it again.

```
Chapter 3
```

November

MISS RASMUSSEN. FIFTH-GRADE TEACHER

Every so often I have one of the parents come into
the class and talk about what they do for a living.
Sam was very proud of his father, and he brought
him in to talk about the military. It was quite interesting, really.

JUDY DOUGLAS. GRADE 5

Snik's dad came in with his uniform and a gun
and everything. Can you imagine? A gun in school?
I thought it was horrible. Why did we have to learn
about war and killing?

SAM DAWKINS. GRADE 5

Judy was all obnoxious, saying the world
would be a better place if we just had peace and

all that hippie stuff. My dad was cool about it. He told her that sometimes a nation has to defend itself and if you don't your enemies will just roll over you. She says that all war wasn't like that, and he told her some is. What did she know about war, anyway? He really told her off.

MISS RASMUSSEN, FIFTH-GRADE TEACHER

I thought it was a wonderful debate. Arguments are not necessarily bad things. They allow people to hear other points of view. The students were really into it. I let them form their own opinions.

KELSEY DONNELLY, GRADE 5

Snik's dad and Judy went at it for like a long time. It was great. We got to miss math.

SAM DAWKINS, GRADE 5

I walk into class one day and the first person I see is Kelsey. Her hair is pink! *Pink!* Who dyes their hair pink? She looked like a cartoon character or something. Man, you dye your hair pink and you might as well just carry a big sign that says, PAY ATTENTION TO ME! I couldn't believe it.

JUDY DOUGLAS. GRADE 5

Snik told me to get a load of Kelsey, and I saw that hideous hair. At first I thought she used that spray-on stuff and it washes off in a week or so. But it was the real thing! Can you imagine?

Well, I thought it was just awful at first. I can't imagine why anyone would want to deface themselves like that. I can't imagine anyone's parent letting a child our age do that. I thought about it some more, though. It occurred to me that I don't like it when people judge me by the color of my skin. I shouldn't judge anyone by the color of their hair.

KELSEY DONNELLY. GRADE 5

So I dyed my hair. Big whup. They all acted like I cut off my arm or something. It was a birthday present. My mom dyes her hair so she'll look younger, so she couldn't really argue that I wanted to dye my hair. Whatever. I thought you wanted to know about the homework machine.

MISS RASMUSSEN. FIFTH-GRADE TEACHER

Fifth grade is hard. Kids have to express their individuality. Pink hair, blue hair, it doesn't matter to me. As long as they pay attention, complete their assignments, and try their best, they can do what they want with their hair.

Our school goes all the way from K to grade twelve, but the older grades have their own part of the building. When they reach fifth grade, the kids almost think they rule the school. You know what I mean. They're going to be moving up to middle school, where they will be the "little kids" again. They want to enjoy being top dogs while they still can. Some of them, anyway.

I really didn't see much of a difference during the first marking period. Sam was struggling, with both his grades and his attitude. Kelsey was doing okay, but not great. Judy scored in the nineties on all her assignments. Brenton never got less than a hundred.

I told the kids what I always tell them. Hard work pays off. The harder you work, the better you will do. I think that applies to everything in life.

SAM DAWKINS, GRADE 5

Well, right away I decide that I *have* to find a way to use the homework machine to do my homework for me. Why not? When cars were invented, people didn't keep using their horses and buggies, did they? When the telephone was invented, people didn't keep sending telegrams. When the computer was invented, people gave up their typewriters. Same thing here.

I wanted to keep it between me and Brenton, but Judy and Kelsey already knew about the homework machine, so I had to include them.

JUDY DOUGLAS. GRADE 5

It was Snik who called a meeting with Kelsey and me in the playground after school one day. It was like he had his whole speech all planned out. He said there were only four people in the whole world who knew about the homework machine. The three of us and Brenton, of course. He said we should keep it that way. I asked him what he had in mind. That was when he said we should all use the homework machine to do our homework.

Well, I didn't like the idea at all. I get A's. I've made the honor roll every year. I don't need any machine to do my homework for me. I don't need any help.

Snik said to me, "Sure you get A's. But you have to work so hard to get them. Wouldn't you like to take it easy a little? Wouldn't you like to have more time to do other things besides homework? For all your work, you're still only the *second* smartest kid in the class. Brenton is the smartest, and he doesn't have to do any homework at *all*. He's got a machine that does it for him. Is that fair to you?"

Snik may not be the smartest kid in the world, but he's a good talker. He got me thinking. Maybe Brenton got better grades than me because he had a machine doing his homework for him. That's not exactly fair. The playing field wasn't level.

After thinking it over for a long time I said okay, let's talk to Brenton and see if he'll let us use the homework machine.

KELSEY DONNELLY, GRADE 5

I said sure, whatever. Include me in. There's nothing good on TV after school anyway.

SAM DAWKINS, GRADE 5

So I figure Brenton's not going to just let us use his machine for free. What would be in it for him? We would have to pay him or give him something. That's only fair. But I don't have any money. So I think, what does this kid need more than anything else? What does he not have?

And the answer is obvious. He doesn't have

friends. Maybe he'd let us use the homework machine if we became his friends.

BRENTON DAMAGATCHI, GRADE 5

When Snik came up to me during recess and said he wanted to talk about the homework machine, I had a bad feeling in the pit of my stomach. I thought he was going to blackmail me. I thought he was going to tell me that unless I let him use the homework machine, he was going to tell Miss Rasmussen about it and get me in trouble.

But he didn't say that at all. Instead, he said that if I let him use the homework machine to do his homework, he would be my friend. As if the one thing in the world that I really wanted was for Sam Dawkins to be my friend.

SAM DAWKINS, GRADE 5

Well, Brenton just laughs in my face. He says, "I don't need friends." He says, "You don't have to be my friend. If you want to use the homework machine, that's fine. Just come over anytime and use it." He doesn't ask for anything in return.

I didn't get it. He could have gotten just about *anything* out of me. For all his smarts, the guy just didn't know how to cut a deal. Fine with me. That was the way I looked at it. If somebody's gonna give you something for nothing, take it.

JUDY DOUGLAS, GRADE 5

The three of us rode our bikes over to Brenton's house after school that day. His mom kind of looked at us like she couldn't believe we were back. She made us popcorn and some of those slice-and-bake cookies with designs on them. They were yummy.

It was all so easy. Miss Rasmussen had given us a worksheet with a bunch of questions about the Grand Canyon on it. We didn't even bother looking anything up. Brenton just slipped the worksheet in the scanner and a few minutes later the worksheet popped out of the printer with the answers on it. Like magic.

Brenton had each of us produce a handwriting sample, and he scanned our handwriting into the computer. Then he programmed it to print out separate sheets with the answers printed in our own handwriting. It was impossible to tell that we hadn't filled out the worksheets ourselves. Our homework was done in no time.

KELSEY DONNELLY, GRADE 5

When Brenton gave me my worksheet with the answers on it, I pulled a dollar out of my backpack and handed it to him. I figured the least I could do was give him a buck for doing my homework for me and saving me an hour of work. But he wouldn't take it. He said don't be silly.

We used him. I admit it. We used him all year long. But it's not like he got nothing out of it. We had some fun.

SAM DAWKINS, GRADE 5

So we were over Brenton's house and I see that he has a chessboard on his desk. I wonder who he plays. I mean, the kid had no friends. So he says, "I play against myself."

He would actually play the black pieces *and* the white pieces against each other, and take turns playing both sides. Do you believe that? It sounded nuts to me.

He asks me if I play and I say no way. He says he would teach me how to play if I want to learn but I say no thanks, that game is boring.

I didn't tell him, but I figured there's no way a dummy like me could learn a game that complicated and play a genius like him. I don't like losing. I've got a reputation to uphold.

KELSEY DONNELLY, GRADE 5

We went over Brenton's house to do our homework the next day too. And after a while we were going over there every day.

BRENTON'S MOM

I was so pleased that Brenton was forming this small group of friends. Finally!

The kids always kept the door closed. I assumed they were doing their homework together and they needed to concentrate. I didn't ask a lot of questions. I was just happy that Brenton was beginning to fit in.

BRENTON DAMAGATCHI, GRADE 5

While we waited for the pages to come out of the printer, Snik kept looking over at my chessboard. I remembered how he showed so much enthusiasm when we were building catapults in October, and he was always talking about his dad in the military and war and things like that.

So I said well you know, chess is essentially a virtual simulation of war. He seemed to be unaware of that. He thought it was a slow, boring game for "eggheads."

I explained to him that when you play chess, you're like a general with a whole army of all kinds of soldiers at your command. It's not at all like checkers, where you just jump over the enemy. In chess, you get to attack and destroy the enemy. You try to hunt down and trap the opposing king while making sure your own king is safe. It's actually very exciting.

I showed him how the various pieces moved. How the bishops slash across the board and kill. How the queen can do just about anything and is all-powerful, but the king is very limited and must be protected. How the pawns are your foot soldiers on the front lines who protect the more powerful pieces and sometimes must be sacrificed for the greater good. I believe he was intrigued.

JUDY DOUGLAS, GRADE 5

I don't remember whose idea it was, but somebody said we needed a nickname for the homework machine. We needed a code name so we wouldn't have to say "the homework machine" out loud in front of other people.

I wanted to call it Doris, myself. Snik said the

homework machine wasn't a *girl*. We had this big argument about whether or not a boy's computer had to have a boy's name or not.

We tried to think of all the names that could be a boy's name *or* a girl's name. You know, Pat. Chris. Casey. Nicky. Randy. Alex. Jamie. Jordan.

Then Snik let out this really loud burp and we all laughed. After we finished saying what a disgusting pig Snik was, Brenton suggested we nickname the homework machine Belch.

I thought it was a little crude, but the others thought it was perfect. So from that moment on, we started to call the homework machine Belch.

KELSEY DONNELLY, GRADE 5

I said fine. Belch. Whatever you want to call it is fine with me. As long as it works.

SAM DAWKINS, GRADE 5

My dad had an old chessboard in the bookcase. So I pull it out one night and put the pieces on the squares. No way I was gonna try to play in front of a genius like Brenton, but it was kinda cool fooling around with it. Brenton was right. The game is a lot like war, but in slow motion.

JUDY DOUGLAS, GRADE 5

I knew from the start that what we were doing was wrong. In the back of my mind, anyway. There was no question about that. I should have stopped everything before it ever got started. But I didn't. The only thing that I thought about back then was making sure we didn't get caught.

We had an informal agreement that Belch would be our little secret, but I thought it should be more official. So all four of us put our hands together and promised not to tell anybody, *anybody* about Belch.

If any kid ever found out, we agreed, the person who leaked the secret would be doomed for the rest of his or her life, and afterward, too. They would live a horrible, unhappy existence and they'd get straight F's on their report cards and they'd never go to college and all their pets would get run over by SUVs. And if anybody's parents ever found out, well, you could just forget about your childhood. It would be over.

Everybody agreed, and then we played kickball.

MISS RASMUSSEN, FIFTH-GRADE TEACHER

I noticed sometime in November that the D Squad seemed to be coming together as a unit.

They were very different in background and so many other ways, but they seemed to be becoming friends. They gravitated toward one another during lunch and recess. They left school at the end of the day as a group.

I was very pleased. It's so rare to see a boy like Sam forming a friendship with a boy like Brenton or a girl like Kelsey bonding with a girl like Judy.

Looking back, I feel like a fool. How could I have been so blind?

BRENTON DAMAGATCHI, GRADE 5

About a month after I got that mysterious e-mail, I got another message. I had completely forgotten about him, until I saw the name at the bottom: Milner. This time, the guy sent me an instant message. He asked me what part of the country I lived in, and what kind of computer equipment I used. He said he would pay me if I answered his questions. I didn't feel comfortable. I probably should have told my parents. But I didn't particularly want them to know about Belch. I changed my screen name and e-mail address.

Chapter 4

December

SAM DAWKINS. GRADE 5

So Brenton keeps asking me if I wanna play chess with him, and I keep saying no because I know he'd beat the snot out of me and I don't like losing. But I did think the game was cool, and my dad said he'd teach me how to play. He wasn't an expert or anything, but he was pretty good.

So Dad says you wanna play a game and I say okay and he says I could be white because white goes first and I'm a beginner.

I didn't really know what to do. For my opening move I push the pawn in front of my right knight two squares forward. Dad moves the pawn in front of his king two squares forward. This didn't look so hard. So I move the pawn in front of my right bishop forward one square. Then Dad slides his queen diagonally all the way to the edge of the board and he says, "Checkmate."

I say, "What?!" He says, "You heard me. Checkmate."

I ask him how he could checkmate me in just two moves and he says look at your king. So I look at my king. He's right. My king can't go anywhere. He's stuck. Two stinking moves and my king was a dead man. The game was over.

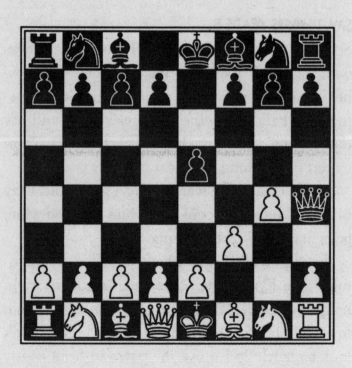

I say to myself he's never gonna do that to me again.

BRENTON DAMAGATCHI, GRADE 5

I never thought Belch was such a big deal, the way the others did. It was just a tool to make a job easier, like a hammer or a screwdriver. It never interested me very much.

What interests me? I'll tell you what interests me. When a whole bunch of people all start doing the same thing at the same time for no apparent reason. That interests me. It's psychology, I guess.

I found it fascinating that all the boys would suddenly come to school wearing backward baseball caps. Or that all the girls would start wearing ankle bracelets or ponytails. Why? Those things have to start somewhere, right? Somebody somewhere has to be the first one to do something. I thought it would be interesting to create a fad.

So I designed this software program. It was fairly simple. It took the words "wear red socks to school on Thursday" and duplicated it and inserted it randomly into documents. I guess you'd call it a virus because I sort of let it loose all over the Internet and people passed it around. I didn't tell anyone at school about it. I just did it for the fun of it.

KELSEY DONNELLY, GRADE 5

I was in a chat room one night and somebody said something about wearing red socks to school. It sounded like a cool idea and everybody said they would do it, and we'd all tell our friends to do it too.

MISS RASMUSSEN, FIFTH-GRADE TEACHER

Every so often we have a "Funny Hair Day" or "Silly Hat Day" at school. But when I came in one Thursday, just about every student in the class was wearing red socks. In fact, just about every student in the whole *school* was wearing red socks. That was curious. I didn't recall receiving a memo about it or a flyer that was sent home in the kids' backpacks. It couldn't have been merely a coincidence.

So I asked the kids why they were wearing red socks and they said somebody sent them an e-mail or an instant message or they read it on the Internet. When I came home that night and turned on the TV news, there was a report that kids all over America had worn red socks to school. It didn't mean anything. It was just for the fun of it.

There was only one student in my class who, I noticed, wasn't wearing red socks that day. It was Brenton.

SAM DAWKINS. GRADE 5

Sure I wore red socks. Everybody did. Except for Brenton. I figured, of course not. Brenton's out of it. He probably didn't get the word.

JUDY DOUGLAS. GRADE 5

We were over Brenton's house doing our homework after school that day. I remember we were talking about the whole red socks thing while waiting for the printer to finish. Everybody had on red socks except for Brenton, so I asked him why he didn't wear red socks. I figured he just never paid attention to fashions or things like that. But he made this cute little smile and we knew something was up because he doesn't usually smile that much. We made him tell us, and he admitted that *he* was the one who started the whole red socks fad in the first place. Can you imagine?

SAM DAWKINS. GRADE 5

The red socks thing blew my mind! Think of it. This one kid took his computer and with a few keystrokes got just about everybody in America to do this dumb thing. It was cool! And that kid was sitting next to me. Think of the power! He could make every kid in America hop backward and recite the "Pledge of Allegiance" if he wanted to.

KELSEY DONNELLY. GRADE 5

I remember the night of red socks day, everybody online was chatting about how cool it was. I couldn't resist. I told everybody I knew the guy who started the whole thing. I didn't mention Brenton's name. Right away, I got an IM from a guy asking me who pulled off red socks day. I didn't tell him. I didn't think Brenton wanted everybody to know. The guy gave me his name and an e-mail address in case I changed my mind. The name was Milner.

JUDY DOUGLAS. GRADE 5

One of the nicest things about Belch was that I had more time after school. I asked my mom if I could take a ballet class on Wednesdays and she said sure, as long as I still had time to do my homework. Before we had Belch, I spent just about every day after school doing my homework. There was no time for anything else.

SAM DAWKINS, GRADE 5

Sometimes, when I was sitting at home playing video games or watching TV or just hanging out, I would think about the other saps in my class who were doing homework right then. Ha! Suckers! This is the life. I felt like I won the lottery or something.

RONNIE TEOTWAWKI, GRADE 5

I had been watching those D Squad jerks from across the room. I knew something was up way back in December. One day I saw Snikwad, who is relatively cool, walking home from school with that dweeb Brenton Damagatchi. What was up with that? No way the two of them could be friends. Not in a million years. It didn't make sense. I was suspicious. Something was up. I just didn't know what.

JUDY DOUGLAS, GRADE 5

I thought that I would just try Brenton's machine a few times and then go back to doing my homework the old-fashioned way. But I realized that I *liked* not having to work so hard on my homework. I liked the extra free time I had. It was so easy to just slip the homework assignment into the scanner and watch the finished homework come out the other end a few minutes later.

It was like microwave popcorn. My mom told me that when she was a girl, they popped popcorn in a big pot on the stove with oil, and it was greasy and hard to clean up. Now she makes popcorn in the microwave, and she says she would never go back to the old way. That was how I was starting to feel about homework.

SAM DAWKINS. GRADE 5

My dad said that if we played a game of chess every night, I would get better and better. So we started playing every night.

The first thing Dad told me is that wars aren't won or lost because of guns and soldiers and shooting. They're won or lost because of strategy. He said the way to win is to build a strong position by slowly accumulating advantages. Like, you want to try to control the four squares in the center of the board.

It was little things like that. Stuff you don't normally think of. Like, when your king is in the middle of the board, he has eight squares he can escape to. But when he's at the edge of the board, he has just five squares he can escape to. And if he's in the corner, he only has three squares. He's just about dead.

KELSEY DONNELLY, GRADE 5

I was hanging around doing nothing and my mother starts in giving me a hard time. "When are you going to do your homework, Kelsey?" And all that. So I told her I did it already, over at Brenton's house.

Well, she doesn't believe me, of course. She says, "If you're lying, you're grounded, young lady." So I showed her my homework and she looks it over real carefully. Finally she says I did a good job and if I kept it up like that she would let me pierce my belly button. Ha! It was great.

BRENTON DAMAGATCHI, GRADE 5

After we finished doing everybody's homework, they went home. They didn't usually hang around, and that was fine with me. I had my own projects to work on.

Every so often I would ask Snik if he wanted to play a game of chess, but he always turned me down. He said he had a dentist appointment or he wasn't feeling well or something. I knew that it was just an excuse. He didn't like me enough to get together unless we were doing our homework. That was fine. As I said, I really don't need or have time for friends. But it did please my mother to think they were my friends, and I like to please my mother. After a while, I stopped asking Snik to play.

JUDY DOUGLAS. GRADE 5

Every so often I would stay after we finished our homework. Unlike most boys, you can talk to Brenton about things other than sports and motorcycles and dumb things like that. I could bring up something about, say, classical music or politics, and he would be able to discuss it. Nobody else was like that. Brenton knows about everything. He's like an encyclopedia.

MISS RASMUSSEN. FIFTH-GRADE TEACHER

It was getting close to the holidays and I noticed that the kids in the D Squad were doing remarkably well. I certainly expected it from Brenton and Judy, but Sam and Kelsey were working on A's in all their subjects, which was a surprise. Their parents thought I was a miracle worker.

In the back of my mind, I suspected that Sam and Kelsey might be copying off Brenton and Judy. But I wanted to believe that all my lessons about hard work were starting to pay off. Now, of course, I realize I was just fooling myself.

KELSEY'S MOM

When Kelsey brought home her end-of-the-year report card with all A's and B's on it, I just about fell off my chair. She had always been a C student. I figured there had to be some kind of mistake. I thought Miss Rasmussen switched the report cards around or something.

KELSEY DONNELLY, GRADE 5

My mom said that because my report card was so good, I could get my belly button pierced. We drove over to the place, but I chickened out at the last minute. It was too scary. I couldn't go through with it.

SAM DAWKINS, GRADE 5

So I thought of a great idea. You know how McDonald's and Burger King and all those other fast-food joints are in just about every town? Well, what if there was a Belch in every town? Kids could go there after school to get their homework done. That would be cool.

Kids could ride in with their bikes, drop off their homework assignment at the first window, and then ride up to the second window a few minutes later to pick up their finished homework. We could call it McHomework.

Just think of it! There are millions of kids in the United States. If each of those kids paid a dollar a day to get their homework done, we would be rich. We would be richer than Bill Gates!

JUDY DOUGLAS, GRADE 5

Snik told us about his harebrained idea to franchise Belch and have kids ride their bikes up to the drive-through window like it was a fast-food restaurant. I told him he was out of his mind. If any parents ever found out about Belch, it would be all over. Nobody would *ever* let their kids go to a place like that.

He admitted I was right and said, "Well, it was a good idea while it lasted." Yeah, and it lasted about three minutes. I also reminded him that we had a pact to keep the whole thing a secret.

Sometime in October, I noticed a subtle shift in the way the other students were acting toward me. It appeared that they were no longer calling me "dork" or "nerd" or "geek" and they had started to refer to me as "dude."

It was difficult to explain. I certainly had not changed. The only difference in my life, as far as I could see, was that I was often in the company of Snik. So my hypothesis was that other kids thought I was cool because I was with someone who they perceived to be cool. I had become cool by association.

This was easy to test, using the scientific method. I had been compiling data for months. When I plugged it into the computer, the results confirmed my hypothesis.

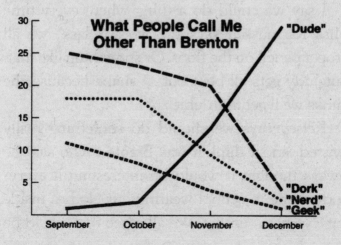

I showed my graph to Snik. He laughed and said, "If you ask me, you're still a dork, dork."

I believe that will change the results of my experiment.

SAM DAWKINS, GRADE 5

I couldn't stop thinking about red socks day and how cool it was. So I tell the others we should start a fad, and they say what kind of fad, and I say I don't know, something really stupid. We start batting around some ideas like green socks day or pink socks day or no-socks day and they all sound lame. Been there, done that.

I say we could do a thing where every time Miss Rasmussen says the word "class" we all drop a pencil on the floor. Or something like that. But Judy gets all bent out of shape because she thinks we'll get in trouble.

Kelsey says we should do something really twisted, and I think it was Brenton who said he always thought it would be interesting if everybody came to school wearing our clothes inside out. No harm in that. We all agree that would be the greatest, so Brenton does his thing with the computer like last time and we go home.

The next day, like every kid in America comes to school with their clothes inside out. It was awesome.

MISS RASMUSSEN, FIFTH-GRADE TEACHER

It was the last day of school before Christmas vacation, I believe. I walked into the class and they were all just sitting there with their hands folded on their desks, grinning these little grins. Then I noticed their clothes.

JUDY DOUGLAS, GRADE 5

Miss Rasmussen just stood there and looked at us. Then she said she had to go to the office. I thought for sure that we were all going to be in big trouble. Maybe we would all be suspended. It was going to totally ruin the holidays.

A few minutes later, she walked back in the class, and she was wearing her clothes inside out! It was the greatest. She's pretty cool for a teacher. We gave her a standing ovation.

KELSEY DONNELLY, GRADE 5

After inside-out day, I got another IM from that Milner guy. He asked me if the same kid who started red socks day had anything to do with inside-out day. He was creeping me out. I told him it was none of his business, and if I ever heard from him again, I would call the police. I also said my dad would find him and beat him up. So he types back, "Kelsey, you don't have a dad." How did *he* know I didn't have a dad? How did he know my name was Kelsey? That *really* creeped me out. I was going to tell everybody about it, but then all that stuff happened with Snik's dad.

Chapter 5

January

SAM DAWKINS. GRADE 5

My dad was sent overseas. It was during the vacation, I remember. We got the call around New Year's Day. Kind of put a damper on the celebration. He had been in the air force for years and we always knew he could be called away at any time, but I guess we just hoped it wouldn't happen. Me and my brothers and my mom were pretty upset.

But he was a soldier, right? You do what you're ordered to do. You know when you sign up that you're going to defend your country one way or another. I understood. I don't really want to talk about it.

Before he went away, my dad gave me his chessboard and some books about chess. He told me to practice up, so when he came home I would be able to give him a good game.

JUDY DOUGLAS, GRADE 5

I was very upset when Snik's dad was sent to the Middle East. We're not best friends or anything, but even so. Snik was all gung-ho G.I. Joe about it. He said, "My dad is going to shoot guys," and that kind of silly macho talk. I was against the war, and I didn't want to see the dad of someone I knew get hurt.

I didn't discuss it with Snik very much. I didn't want him telling me that people who were against the war were traitors and all that. But I'm sure he was thinking about his dad all the time. How could you not?

BRENTON DAMAGATCHI, GRADE 5

I have always thought that instead of fighting wars, the leaders of the two sides should play a game of chess against each other. Whoever wins the game wins the war. Nobody has to die. War is not the answer. Chess is the answer.

KELSEY DONNELLY, GRADE 5

When I heard that Snik's dad had to go to the Middle East, I just started crying. I couldn't stop.

It was like something opened inside of me. Everybody gathered around me and asked me what was wrong. That was the first time I ever told anybody at school that my dad died. I didn't want Snik's dad to die too.

We probably have air force bases in Hawaii and Southern California and cool places like that all over the world. But *he* had to get sent to the one place where there was a war going on. Talk about bad luck.

MISS RASMUSSEN, FIFTH-GRADE TEACHER

When Sam's father was sent overseas, I noticed a change came over him. He didn't crack many jokes anymore. He stopped making fun of people. He was more businesslike, grim even. I tried to talk to him about it, but he obviously didn't want to. I wanted to comfort him. Sometimes you just can't help.

JUDY DOUGLAS, GRADE 5

By January, we were using Belch every day. I had stopped doing my homework on my own entirely. I never even thought about doing it that way anymore. It was so much easier just using Belch.

My mom used to smoke cigarettes when she was younger. I asked her how she started. She said that she tried a cigarette one day just for the fun of it when she was out with some friends who smoked. She didn't like it that much, but a few days later she was with the same people and she had another one. She just wanted to fit in, you know?

Little by little, she started smoking a cigarette here and there, and soon she started thinking about having a cigarette when she wasn't smoking one. Before she knew it, she was smoking a pack of cigarettes every day, and she was addicted to them. I think I was becoming addicted to Belch almost the same way.

I asked my mom how she quit smoking, and she said it was very hard. She tried a whole bunch of times, but she couldn't do it. Finally, she quit when she was pregnant with me. She didn't want me to be harmed by the tobacco in her body. That's what it took for her to stop.

RONNIE TEOTWAWKI, GRADE 5

Every day, Snikwad, Kelsey, Judy, and Brenton would leave school together. The little foursome. They just *couldn't* be a tight group. I couldn't resist. I had to find out what was going on. So I followed them, hiding behind trees and bushes and stuff so they wouldn't see me.

They went over Brenton's house. I hid behind a car parked across the street. A few minutes after they went inside, I saw some movement in one of the windows on the second floor. It was probably Brenton's bedroom. His mother brought them something on a tray. Then she left and they closed the door.

It looked like Brenton was fussing with his computer. I couldn't tell exactly what he was doing. The others were standing around, talking and laughing. They stayed maybe an hour and then they left. That was it.

SAM DAWKINS, GRADE 5

My dad sent me an e-mail saying how about a game of chess? I ask him how we can play chess when I'm in Arizona and he's in the middle of some desert. He says we should each set up a chessboard and we can tell the other one our moves by e-mail. He says lots of the soldiers are doing it, and he gave me the address of a Web site that makes it easy.

I went to the Web site, but it looked complicated. They use a code to identify the pieces and their positions on the board. It's like this: P = pawn, R = rook, N = knight, B = bishop, Q = queen, and K = king. You use capital letters for the white pieces and lowercase letters for the black pieces. When you're ready to make a move, you name the piece and the square you're moving it to. So if white types in Nf3, that means he's moving his knight to the third row and the sixth column.

I e-mail my dad and say it sounds pretty complicated to me. He says I'm a big wimp and afraid to play him because I know I'd lose. So this is what I e-mail him back: Pe4.

JUDY DOUGLAS, GRADE 5

Jessica Martin used to be my best friend in the whole world. We've known each other since we were in kindergarten. When we were in the same class at school last year, we would come home every day and do our homework together. Sometimes other girls in the class joined us, too.

Jessica asked me to meet her in the bathroom after lunch. She was all serious, like she had something very important and personal to get off her chest. She said she was upset because we hadn't seen each other in a long time and I never called her anymore. I said it was nothing. We were in different classes now, and I was just busy, that's all. I couldn't tell her about Belch, of course.

Jessica asked me if Kelsey was my new best friend, because she saw me riding bikes home from school with her. Jessica said that Kelsey is, like, trailer trash and she's got pink hair and everything.

I said don't be ridiculous. I could never be friends with Kelsey. It wasn't a nice thing to say, but I didn't know what else to say to Jessica. I didn't feel good about the whole thing. I didn't know what to do. I'm just not good in situations like that.

SAM DAWKINS, GRADE 5

So this jerk Ronnie Teotwawki comes up to me in the lunchroom one day and asks me why I'm hanging around with Brenton. I tell him I'm not hanging around with Brenton, and he says oh yeah, how come you leave school with him every day? I say it's none of his business who I leave school with and he better leave me alone and stop watching me or I'll bust his head open. That shut him up.

KELSEY DONNELLY. GRADE 5

My friend Heather in the other class asked me if I wanted to come over after school and listen to this cool new CD she burned by some new band. I told her I couldn't, but I didn't tell her I was going over to Brenton's house with Judy and Snik.

She looked kinda hurt and said what's up? How come I see you with that jerk Judy all the time now? Are you friends? Are you turning goody-goody? She said Judy was stuck-up and snotty and all that. I said I know. I told her I wasn't friends with Judy or anything. I couldn't tell Heather about Belch. She tells everybody everything. I guess it's better for Heather to tell everybody I'm friends with Judy than to have her tell everybody about Belch.

JUDY DOUGLAS. GRADE 5

I felt bad about Jessica, so I called her up and asked her if she wanted to do something. She said she couldn't because she had a ton of homework to do. My homework was done hours before. She started asking all these questions, like how come you aren't working on your homework? How did you finish it so fast?

I kind of freaked out. What was I supposed to

say? That a machine did my homework *for* me? I told Jessica that I did some of my homework at school, but I'm not sure if she believed me.

I was never very good at lying. Some people can just look you in the eye and tell you a total lie and you never know it. When I tell a lie, I get nervous and I start sweating and stuttering and I can't look the person in the face. I'm terrible at it. I'd rather just tell the truth, to tell you the truth. But sometimes you can't.

KELSEY DONNELLY, GRADE 5

Heather said she thought it over and she couldn't be friends with me anymore if I was going to hang out with a stuck-up jerk like Judy. So I told her that I didn't want to be friends with anybody who insisted on telling me who I was allowed to hang out with. She got all mad and so did I. I guess me and Heather aren't friends anymore.

JUDY DOUGLAS, GRADE 5

I was walking to the bike rack with Snik and Kelsey when I saw Jessica and some of the other girls leaving school together. I guess they were going to go do their homework together.

Jessica kind of glanced at me. She didn't invite me to join them. She didn't say anything. Neither did I. After that we weren't friends anymore.

MISS RASMUSSEN, FIFTH-GRADE TEACHER

When Sam told me he was playing a game of chess with his father by e-mail, I was just thrilled. Before that, I didn't see that he had any real hobbies or interests. Finally he had found a positive interest that would stimulate his mind, and every child needs that. For some kids, it's sports, or playing a musical instrument, or reading. For me, it was nature. For Sam, it was chess.

I also thought playing chess was a great way for him to keep in touch with his father, who was so far away. It helped get Sam out of his funk for a while, too.

I was careful not to tell Sam how pleased I was with the chess, though. Sam is one of those students who think that if a grown-up approves of something they do, it must not be very cool and maybe he should stop doing it. I didn't want that to happen. You have to be very careful with the way you treat each child.

JUDY DOUGLAS, GRADE 5

My dad has this thing where we have to sit around the dinner table and talk about serious subjects every night. Like, he'll bring up the subject of gun control or athletes taking steroids and the whole family has to give our opinions.

One night we were talking about knowing right from wrong. Dad said that sometimes the difference between right and wrong is obvious. Like when you add two numbers together, there is a right answer and a wrong answer. Or robbing a bank or killing somebody is definitely wrong.

But in some situations, you can't tell the difference between right and wrong so easily. Like driving faster than the speed limit is wrong, but if you're rushing to the hospital so that a baby can be born, then speeding is okay. Or hitting somebody with a baseball bat is wrong, but if that person was attacking your mom, then it's okay.

I didn't feel well. I felt physically ill. I had to excuse myself from the table.

KELSEY DONNELLY, GRADE 5

Feeling guilty about what we did? Yeah, I guess a little. But hey, we didn't hurt anybody. There are a lot of horrible people in the world who get away with lots of stuff. What we did wasn't so bad. There are degrees of wrongness, you know? If you get all worked up over the little wrongs, you won't appreciate how wrong the big wrongs are.

POLICE CHIEF REBECCA FISH

I first became aware of this so-called homework machine back in January. Got an anonymous tip. Somebody called the hotline and said a kid at Grand Canyon School developed a machine that did homework automatically. Then they hung up. It sounded like a kid. Traced the call to a pay phone. Figured it was a crank. Kids do this kind of stuff all the time. Sounded like a load of bull, if you'll excuse my French.

It's standard procedure to keep a record of all calls. So I did, of course. Just in case. I know a guy in Washington who looks into this kind of stuff. Told him what I knew, which wasn't much. He said maybe he would check it out if he had time.

RONNIE TEOTWAWKI, GRADE 5

It wasn't me. I swear it wasn't me who told the cops about the machine. I'll swear it on a stack of Bibles if you want me to. I'll swear it on my mother. I never called the police.

Chapter 6

February

JUDY DOUGLAS. GRADE 5

One morning Kelsey came to me and said she had a secret she wanted to share with me. Ordinarily, I don't like sharing secrets or hearing other people's secrets. It's not that far from lying, really, because once you know someone's secret and you keep it to yourself, you're not being honest with the people around you.

Anyway, Kelsey looked like she was going to tell me the secret no matter what. She lifts up her shirt and shows me that she had pierced her belly button.

Well, I almost threw up. That is just about the most disgusting thing I ever saw. I can't believe her mom would let her do that. Or maybe I can. After all, she did let Kelsey dye her hair pink. But

I can't understand why anybody would ever want to do that. It's just gross.

My mom always told me that if I don't have something nice to say to somebody, I should say nothing at all. But I lied and told Kelsey her belly button ring was cool. I didn't want to hurt her feelings.

KELSEY DONNELLY, GRADE 5

I knew Judy thought that what I did was disgusting. She's good at a lot of stuff, but she's not very good at hiding her feelings. But hey, she pierced her ears, right? What's the difference?

MISS RASMUSSEN, FIFTH-GRADE TEACHER

I was in the lounge and I asked some of the other teachers if it was common for an unpopular child to suddenly become popular with the other students. That's what seemed to have happened with Brenton. He was just about shunned when school started, and very soon he seemed to be quite popular. I couldn't figure it out.

Mrs. Wallace, who has been teaching for more than twenty years, said that a child can change a lot in one year. Some kids start fifth grade at the maturity level of a fourth grader and end the year with the maturity level of a sixth grader. But she said that in all her years of teaching she had only seen unpopular kids suddenly become popular a few times. She said that if that happens, it means the other kids are using him or her in some way. Kids don't just suddenly become popular for no reason.

JUDY DOUGLAS, GRADE 5

One day I went to get a drink of water after the bell rang for dismissal, and when I got back to class, Snik, Brenton, and Kelsey were gone. They went to Brenton's house without me! That had never happened before. I was really upset.

I hopped on my bike and all the way over there I was trying to figure it out. Was it an accident? Or did they do it on purpose? Maybe there was something they wanted to talk about and they didn't want me to hear. Were they trying to send me a message? Were they trying to cut me out of the group? I didn't know what to do.

KELSEY DONNELLY, GRADE 5

Judy came in all upset. I asked her what was wrong and she said nothing. But it was so obvious. It was all over her face. She totally can't hide her emotions. Finally she blurted out that she was mad because we left without her.

Man, she gets upset easy! I told her it was nothing. We looked around for her after school and couldn't find her, so we left. What's the big deal? I told her she was being silly, and then she got mad at *that*. Her voice was even trembling.

She stayed mad for a long time. Man, when she grows up, she's gonna get an ulcer or something. She cares too much about everything. She's lucky she doesn't have anything *serious* to worry about.

When I was six, my dad got hit by a snowmobile and he died. I was there. I saw it. When something like that happens to you, it puts stuff into perspective. I'm not going to get all bent out of shape because some kids leave school without me. You know what I mean?

SAM DAWKINS. GRADE 5

In an e-mail, I asked my dad if he shot anybody yet. He said he didn't want to talk about stuff like that, and maybe we should stick to chess.

He beat me pretty fast in that first e-mail game. I guess I wasn't paying close enough attention because he captured my queen and after that he just took all my other pieces one by one. I'll never let that happen again.

After he checkmates me, he asks me if I'm up for another game or am I too chicken? I tell him to bring it on, hotshot. He moves one of his pawns up and so do I. I move the pieces on our chessboard at home, so I can see the game better.

Chess by e-mail is pretty cool. I would usually check my mail after dinner and Dad's move would be there waiting for me. I liked having as much time as I needed to decide what to do next. No pressure.

I learned some of the basic strategy by then. Like, you want to bring your pieces out from the back row as early in the game as possible. But you don't want to bring your queen out too early, because then she's open to attack and she can get in the way of your pawns. It's a really complicated game. You gotta think.

BRENTON DAMAGATCHI, GRADE 5

Snik came in one morning with his chessboard. He told me he was playing a game against his dad and he needed some advice. He set up the pieces and I looked things over. He had done a pretty nice job. His dad was a piece ahead, but Snik was in a good position and could still win.

I told him a few things he didn't know. Like a rook is worth more than a bishop or knight, which are worth about the same. And if you have two pawns in position to make a capture, you want to capture toward the center of the board. But he had already learned a lot of stuff on his own. He's smarter than he gives himself credit for.

I'm an okay player. Not great. I've never really studied the game. The most important thing to know is that chess isn't a battle, it's a war. You want to gradually build up tiny advantages and make your position better until the enemy has no choice but to quit. I advised Snik to castle so he could get his king away from the center of the board.

MISS RASMUSSEN, FIFTH-GRADE TEACHER

I really didn't know all that much about chess myself. I had played a tiny bit as a child. All I knew was how the various pieces moved. I didn't understand strategy.

But when I saw Sam and Brenton talking over a chessboard, it seemed like one of those wonderful teachable moments we live for. So I scrapped our lesson plan for the morning. I drew the chessboard on the chalkboard and explained to everyone the basic rules of play.

The students started giving their ideas about which move Sam should make next. Sam and Brenton stood at the front of the class and explained why some moves might be smarter than others. It was fascinating for the whole class! I could almost see the wheels turning in their little heads.

We spent the whole morning doing that, and finally Sam decided to castle. That's when your king and rook sort of switch places.

It was a wonderful learning experience that I'll remember for the rest of my teaching career.

JUDY'S MOM

I couldn't help but notice that Judy wasn't spending much time doing homework. In fourth grade, she used to come home from school and work on it for *hours*. Even if she didn't have too much homework, she would go over it again and again until it was perfect.

I naturally assumed that her workload would be a little heavier in fifth grade, but that wasn't the case. It seemed like she never did any homework at *all*. I was worried. Maybe she had lost her enthusiasm for school.

I asked Judy about it and she said that Miss Rasmussen was a really easy teacher who didn't believe in giving a lot of homework. When we had our parent-teacher conference, I suggested to Miss Rasmussen that maybe she should give the students more homework. She told me that some of the students felt there was too much homework as it was, and a few of the parents had complained about the time their kids had to spend on it.

She said that Judy was just an excellent student, and that was probably why she finished her homework so quickly. I wanted to believe that, and so I did.

KELSEY DONNELLY, GRADE 5

Then there was the day Judy made a Valentine's Day card for Brenton, and it was like World War III broke out.

SAM DAWKINS, GRADE 5

So Judy gives a Valentine's Day card to Brenton. She doesn't give one to me. She doesn't give one to Kelsey. I don't think she gave one to anybody in the class but Brenton. Maybe she only gives Valentines to the smart kids.

I wasn't jealous. I mean, a girl has the right to like anybody she wants. It just kind of took me by surprise, that's all. I didn't know she liked Brenton. Actually, I kind of thought she might have a crush on *me*. I can't imagine why she would pick him over me.

JUDY DOUGLAS, GRADE 5

I didn't *like* either of them. Snik thinks he is so cool, but deep down he is so insecure. He couldn't get over the idea that anybody might like Brenton better than him.

It meant *nothing*. It was just a silly Valentine. But everybody in the class was talking about it, as if Brenton and I were going to get married or something.

BRENTON DAMAGATCHI, GRADE 5

I have always viewed Valentine's Day, and most holidays for that matter, as artificial celebrations that provide opportunities for big corporations to make people feel guilty and buy greeting cards, flowers, chocolates, and presents. But it was a nice gesture. I thought nothing of it.

KELSEY DONNELLY, GRADE 5

There was this one day when Miss Rasmussen gave us a homework vacation. No homework for a change. Well, when we left school, we all forgot that there was no homework, and headed for Brenton's house anyway like we always did. It wasn't until we got up to his room that we figured out we didn't have any homework to do! We all felt pretty stupid.

We were going to go home, but Brenton's mom brought in some chocolate chip cookies that were awesome. We took them down to the basement and played Ping-Pong for a while.

It turns out that Brenton is a great Ping-Pong player! I couldn't believe it. He even beat Snik, who is always the best athlete in gym. Snik was all mad, and he was saying that Brenton was cheating and stuff. It was a riot. I'll say this for Brenton, he constantly surprises you.

SAM DAWKINS, GRADE 5

I like to hit the ball hard and slam it past the other guy. But Brenton wouldn't let me. He kept dinking these stupid little weak shots just over the net where I couldn't reach them and putting these weird spins on the ball so I wouldn't know which way it was gonna bounce. That's got to be illegal.

RONNIE TEOTWAWKI, GRADE 5

Yeah, I was the one who wrote the message on the boys' room wall. I guess now that it's all over I can admit it. Hey, it wasn't as bad as what *they* did.

I knew they were up to something. No way kids like Judy and Brenton would hang around with kids like Kelsey and Snikwad. Heck, no way *any* of them should hang around with each other. And no way kids like Kelsey and Snikwad should be getting A's.

So I wrote D SQUAD ARE CHEATERS with a marker on the wall of one of the stalls. I used my left hand so nobody could say it was my handwriting. That's all I did. I didn't know how they were cheating, but they had to be doing something. It got rubbed off the next day, but I guess word got around. People were talking.

SAM DAWKINS, GRADE 5

So I'm in the boys' room and I see the graffiti. I scribble over it right away. I hoped that nobody else saw it, but maybe every boy in the school saw it before I went in there. Who knows? I didn't know who wrote it, but I had my suspicions.

The whole thing shook me up. If anybody found out about Belch, we would be in big trouble.

KELSEY DONNELLY, GRADE 5

Snik said we had to have another meeting, so we all met at the big concrete turtle in the playground during recess. We get there and he's all whispering and stuff. Like we're spies. He says we may have a rat. A leak. He wanted to know who spilled the beans. Well, it sure wasn't me, I knew that.

Nobody admitted it. Judy got all freaked out like she was gonna cry or something. She is so emotional! Brenton said one of those weird things he always says that makes no sense to anybody but him.

Snik said we should all be cool about it and remember that we made a pact not to tell *anybody*. He said that if anybody asks any of us about Belch, we should deny everything. Just say none of us knew anything about it.

I figured it was nothing. Kids pass around dumb rumors about other kids all the time. But this time the rumor was true.

MISS RASMUSSEN, FIFTH-GRADE TEACHER

After thinking it over for a long time, I decided to split up the kids in D Squad. I didn't like the way they were always whispering to each other. It's good when a group of kids bonds together, but when they form their own little secret society that excludes everyone else, it's usually a sign of trouble. I suspected something was going on.

I told the class it would be a good learning experience if they changed seats every so often and got to work with other students. I put Sam, Judy, Kelsey, and Brenton in separate groups, one in each corner of the classroom.

KELSEY DONNELLY, GRADE 5

We were constantly having these stupid meetings. It seemed like we had a meeting every day. This time it was Judy who said we had to have one. It was right after Miss Rasmussen changed our seats around and Judy was freaking out, as usual. She was starting to get pimples on her face over this. We met at Brenton's house after school because Judy didn't want us to be seen together at recess. She was all worried.

JUDY DOUGLAS, GRADE 5

Teachers don't just move everybody's desk around for no reason. Usually it's because of a behavior problem. Or maybe they find out that some kid has bad eyesight or hearing and they need to sit closer to the front of the room. But none of that was going on.

None of the other groups were split up the way we were, with each of them stuck in a different corner. Miss Rasmussen did it on purpose. I was sure. She probably figured it all out. She probably knew about Belch. Everything I had worked so hard for was gone. My face was breaking out. I felt like my life was over.

KELSEY DONNELLY, GRADE 5

The phone rang one day when I was home alone. I picked it up and it was that Milner guy! He says he really wants to talk to me. The guy was like a stalker or something. I have no idea how he got my number. I hung up on him.

Chapter 7

March

RONNIE TEOTWAWKI. GRADE 5

When Miss Rasmussen switched everybody's seat around, I was put at the same table as our genius-in-residence, Brenton Damagatchi. So I figured this was perfect! If any of those D Squad jerks was going to spill the beans, it would be him. He couldn't tell a lie to save his life. This would be my chance to get the truth out of him.

I tried to get all buddy-buddy with him first, making like I was his friend. I offered him gum. I asked him if he wanted to hang out after school. I asked him if he wanted to take a hike in the Canyon sometime. I asked him if he wanted to play ball or something.

Nothing. I couldn't get him to crack. He always

had an excuse. Whatever he was hiding, he wasn't saying.

Finally, I just said to him that I knew what he was up to and he'd better let me in on it or I was going to tell everybody. And he says, and what exactly am I up to? I didn't have anything to say, so I just shut up. He had me. That got me mad.

SAM DAWKINS. GRADE 5

Well, I lost again. My dad attacks with his queen and rook at the same time, and it's like there are intersecting laser beams shooting all over the board. My pieces were all locked up and in each other's way.

So I bring my chessboard into class and we all try to think of every possible move I could make to get out of the situation, but it's hopeless. Brenton says I'm in Zugzwang, which means that any move you make only makes your position worse. I had to resign.

Afterward, my dad sends me an e-mail telling me how proud he is of me. He says I put up a good fight. When I was little, I remember, he used to let me win at games and sports. I would beat him all the time. But he said I was getting too old for that, and I have to learn how to handle losing because in the real world sometimes you win and sometimes you lose.

It made me feel good. We started a new game.

MISS RASMUSSEN, FIFTH-GRADE TEACHER

One day I noticed that the homework turned in by Brenton, Kelsey, Judy, and Sam was remarkably similar, except for the handwriting. This was *after* I had switched their seats around. I also noticed that the four of them still left school together at the end of the day.

I don't know why it took me so long to notice the similarities in their work. With so many papers to correct every night, I just didn't make the connection. And their work was so well done. I tend to notice the kids who make a lot of mistakes, not the kids who get everything right.

I hope that after I've been teaching for a few years, I won't be so overwhelmed with work and will be able to pay more attention to things like this.

SAM DAWKINS, GRADE 5

Miss Rasmussen pulls me aside after school one day and says what an awesome job I'm doing on my homework. I say thanks and try to get out of there as fast as possible. But then she asks me if I ever copy off anybody.

Now that I'm looking back on it all, I guess I should have been insulted. I mean, she was basically saying I'm too dumb to do such good work on my own. But I was cheating, so I wasn't too insulted.

I say no, I do not copy off anybody. And that was the truth, technically. I never copied my homework off Brenton or Judy or anybody. I didn't have to. Belch did the homework *for* me. But I didn't tell Miss Rasmussen that.

KELSEY DONNELLY, GRADE 5

The three of them got all bent out of shape after Miss Rasmussen had that talk with Snik. They decided that me and Snik had to start getting some of the answers wrong so it wouldn't look like a machine was doing our homework for us. So now we had to cheat so it wouldn't look like we were cheating! What a hassle. I can make mistakes just fine on my own.

BRENTON DAMAGATCHI, GRADE 5

It became necessary to rewrite the Belch software to program in intentional mistakes at random intervals for Snik and Kelsey's homework. This was an interesting challenge, and I enjoyed it immensely. It's easy to design a machine that will work perfectly all the time. It's harder to design one that will work perfectly just *most* of the time. It goes against the nature of machines.

It reminded me of what they did with Post-it notes. They created an adhesive that was sticky, but not too sticky. If Post-it notes were stickier, they would not serve their purpose. You wouldn't be able to pull them off and stick them somewhere else. They're perfect because they don't work very well. In other words, they're perfect because they fail. That was what I had to accomplish with Belch.

POLICE CHIEF REBECCA FISH

Received a call on Saturday afternoon, March 16. There was a break-in at the house of the Damagatchi boy. Nobody was home at the time. There was a broken basement window. Some minor damage. Nothing was stolen. Didn't look like a professional job. They ran when the alarm went off. It was a prank by a kid, I guess. Happens all the time.

RONNIE TEOTWAWKI, GRADE 5

I didn't try to break into Brenton's house. I don't care how many times you ask me. I didn't do it, and you can't prove that I did.

JUDY DOUGLAS, GRADE 5

We have this school paper called the *Grand Canyon Times*. It's not a real paper. Just some stories and poems that kids write and it's stapled together. It comes out a few times a year.

Anyway, there's a gossip column in there. Usually the gossip is silly stuff like guess who likes so and so. Or which teacher wears a wig. Stuff like that. But right in the middle of the page there was an item about the homework machine. I freaked out.

THE *GRAND CANYON TIMES*

... and rumors are flying around the canyon that certain people in grade five have invented a mysterious machine that does their homework for them! Can you believe that? Where can we get one of those and how much does it cost? ...

SAM DAWKINS, GRADE 5

I freaked when I saw it. Whoever planted that thing in the paper was a real rat. It wasn't me. I figured it couldn't have been Brenton. I wasn't so sure about Judy or Kelsey.

KELSEY DONNELLY, GRADE 5

After the thing was in the paper, we had to have another stupid meeting. Sam tried to get one of us to confess, but nobody did. We decided that we couldn't meet at recess anymore, and we couldn't be seen talking to each other at school. Judy was totally paranoid that we were going to get caught.

RONNIE TEOTWAWKI, GRADE 5

Okay, okay, I was the one who tried to break into Brenton's house. I had to find out what they were up to. What are you gonna do, throw me in jail? I didn't cheat on my homework. And I had nothing to do with the item in the paper. You'll have to pin that on somebody else.

Look, I didn't know if they had a secret machine or not. But it sounded believable. And if they did have a machine, it wasn't fair to the rest of us. Why should I have to sit there for hours doing my homework by hand while somebody else can just push a button and have some machine do it for him? I wasn't the only one who felt that way. I heard other kids talking about it.

BRENTON'S MOM

It was toward the end of March when a stranger knocked at our door one morning. Brenton was at school. This man asked if he could ask me a few questions. First it was simple questions like how many years have I lived in the house and things like that. Then he started asking me what computer equipment we had and what we do with it. I didn't like the whole idea of this stranger asking me these questions and I asked him to kindly leave. I was frightened. I didn't catch his name.

KELSEY DONNELLY, GRADE 5

We had to have another stupid meeting because some guy was snooping around Brenton's house. I wondered if it was that Milner guy who was stalking me. We decided that we had to move Belch. I said I didn't want it at my house. Judy said she didn't want it at her house. So we moved it to Snik's house. What a pain it was carrying all that stuff. The computer must have weighed a ton. We had to put it in a wheelbarrow.

Thinking back on it now, I noticed one weird thing that I never mentioned to anyone. When we unplugged the computer to move it to Snik's house, that little red light didn't go out.

Chapter 8

April

BRENTON'S MOM

I have never known my son to act irrationally. But I must say I was a bit shocked and angry when he gave away all his computer equipment. Sure, my husband gets it for free through his work. But even so, it was thousands of dollars worth of electronics. You don't just give that away. And Brenton loved his computer.

When I asked him why he gave it all away, he sort of shrugged and acted like I couldn't possibly understand. That's not like my son either. I thought he was going through one of those preteenage phases. Maybe this was his way of rebelling against his father. I should have punished him. Should have. You can always say that, can't you? Only later did I find out the real reason he gave his computer away.

SAM'S MOM

I went upstairs to change the sheets one day and there was this fancy computer system sitting on Sam's desk. It was much nicer than the old PC we got from the air force. I asked him where he got it and he said Brenton gave it to him. Well, that didn't sound right. You don't just give somebody something like that. I told Sam he had to give it back, but he said Brenton's father got lots of free computers and he insisted that Brenton didn't want it. I called up Mrs. Damagatchi and she said it was true. She didn't know why Brenton didn't want it anymore. We figured boys will be boys.

SAM DAWKINS. GRADE 5

My dad and I had a pretty hot game. My plan from the opening was to get my pieces onto good squares as soon as I could. I did that, and Dad actually made a few blunders. He let his rook get caught in front of his pawns so they couldn't advance. By the time we reached the middle game, I was two pawns ahead. So I brought out my queen and let her have the run of the board.

Dad always told me that one of the best forms of defense is to attack, so I did. After I captured his rook, he offered to call it a draw. I could have gone for the win, but I guess I just didn't have that killer instinct yet. But I had my first draw.

Dad said I wasn't just a woodpusher anymore. That's what you call a weak player, a woodpusher. We started another game.

MISS RASMUSSEN, FIFTH-GRADE TEACHER

There were all kinds of rumors swirling around, and I wasn't sure how to handle them. You don't want to punish students based on some silly gossip in the school paper or what somebody wrote in a bathroom stall.

I was talking about it in the teachers' lounge, and one of the other teachers suggested I give the class a surprise test. That would tell me how much the students were remembering from their homework. Normally I don't like the whole idea of giving tests for students this age, but it seemed like a good idea.

I made up a multiple-choice test that covered just about everything we had studied all year. The solar system. The explorers. Arizona geography. Everything. The children were a little surprised when I sprung it on them, to say the least.

SAM DAWKINS, GRADE 5

It was totally unfair, I thought. Miss Rasmussen tells us all year long that she doesn't believe in tests. Then, bang, out of nowhere, she hits us with this huge test.

MISS RASMUSSEN, FIFTH-GRADE TEACHER

Well, the class did pretty well as a whole. I was pleased about that. Brenton got every question right. No surprise there. Sam and Kelsey failed completely. Their grades were the worst in the class. It was like they had never seen the material before. But they had been turning in excellent homework. That made me very suspicious. They should have done better.

What was most surprising though, was that Judy got a C. She's an extremely bright girl who turned in perfect homework every night. There was no reason why she shouldn't have done better. I had no choice but to believe the rumors about cheating were true. I was preparing to present the evidence to the principal.

JUDY DOUGLAS, GRADE 5

I couldn't believe I got a C. I never got a C before in my life! I was so ashamed. Instead of bringing the test home to show to my parents, I stuffed it in the back of my locker. If anybody asked where it was, I decided I would pretend it was lost.

As it turned out, I never had to pretend anything. After what happened, I felt silly for even caring about what I got on the test.

KELSEY DONNELLY. GRADE 5

Snik was absent the day we got the test back. I thought maybe he stayed home from school because he knew he failed. But he was absent the next day, too. Then Miss Rasmussen came in after lunch that second day and she was crying. She told us that Snik's father was killed. I started crying. I know what it's like to lose your dad.

SAM DAWKINS. GRADE 5

I'd rather not talk about what happened to my dad. Is that okay?

MISS RASMUSSEN. FIFTH-GRADE TEACHER

I was told that Sam's father was driving an armored vehicle with three other soldiers and it was ambushed in the middle of the night. Sam's father and the soldier sitting next to him in the front seat were killed. The other two soldiers in the back were severely injured.

It was a horrible tragedy, the kind you simply can't prepare for. Sam wasn't the only child who was upset. Kelsey had lost her father when she was younger, and she was distraught. Counselors were brought in to help us all get over our grief. We made cards. We gave Sam lots of hugs when he came back to school. What else could we do? It's not like a wound that will heal in time.

JUDY DOUGLAS, GRADE 5

Brenton and I were very careful about what we said to Snik after his father was killed. He knew how we felt about the war. We didn't want to say anything that might be insensitive. It was just so sad. Snik was the only one who didn't cry. Maybe he got it out of his system at home. We all felt so sorry for him.

KELSEY DONNELLY, GRADE 5

I was so angry! We had met Snik's dad. He came into our class that day and told us what it was like to be a soldier. He was a good guy. Now he was dead. And for what? It wasn't like World

War II, when America had to, like, save the world from Hitler. It was more like Vietnam. It was a war for nothing. And Snik's dad died for nothing. Just like my dad died for nothing when I was little.

It was stupid. I couldn't stop crying. It was like the world stopped turning.

SAM DAWKINS, GRADE 5

Dad and I were in the middle of a game when it happened. I just let the pieces sit there on the squares where they were. I'll never move them, ever. I don't know if there's an afterlife. But if there is, someday my dad and I will finish that game.

MISS RASMUSSEN, FIFTH-GRADE TEACHER

It was a difficult time for everyone that first week after we got the news, especially for Sam and his mother.

Mr. Dawkins' remains were flown back home a few days later. Just about everyone in the school attended the funeral.

After what happened, I couldn't bring myself to go to Principal Wilson with my suspicions of cheating. I just couldn't do it. It was getting close to the end of the year. For better or worse, I decided to let it slide.

JUDY DOUGLAS, GRADE 5

I thought that we wouldn't use Belch after Snik's dad died. It would have been rude to go over his house at a time like that. But Snik invited us over. He needed the company, I guess. And we were all addicted to Belch at that point.

SAM'S MOM

It was an awful time for us after my husband died, of course. But people were so wonderful, coming around to see if we were okay, cooking us dinners, and so on. Sam's friends Brenton and Judy and Kelsey came over every day after school and worked on their homework together up in his room.

One day I walked in without knocking and they all looked at me like I had caught them doing something wrong. But they were just using the computer Brenton had given Sam. I backed out of there and left them alone.

JUDY DOUGLAS, GRADE 5

After the funeral, there were a lot of outsiders around. I don't just mean tourists. I'm talking about official-looking guys with suits or military uniforms. It was creepy.

One day I was riding my bike and one of these guys stopped me. He didn't say anything about Snik's dad. He started asking me questions about computers. My parents always warned me to be careful around strangers. I yelled at the man and told him to leave me alone or I'd scream. I pedaled away as fast as I could go. Now I was really paranoid. The police or FBI were after us for sure.

KELSEY DONNELLY, GRADE 5

Snik was depressed because of his dad, and who could blame him? Brenton's head was up in the clouds somewhere, like always. And Judy was a basket case. I was worried about her the most. She claimed some weird guy stopped her on the street, and he was probably an FBI agent. I thought that maybe she was hallucinating. That girl just can't deal with stress.

Well, *somebody* had to take charge. So I called a meeting. Yeah, me. At my house. The four of us. We had a long talk. There were so many things we had to talk about.

First, I reminded them all that Belch was supposed to make our lives *easier*. But with all the problems and worrying, it made everything harder. We were spending more time worrying about Belch and trying to keep it a secret than we would have if we just did our stupid homework without the stupid machine.

I reminded them all that we had a pact to keep our secret, and that one of us must have spilled the beans. Which one was it? I knew it wasn't me. They all looked at each other for a long time. Judy said it wasn't her. Snik said it wasn't him. We all looked at Brenton. He just looked down and said real quietly, "It was me. I'm sorry."

BRENTON DAMAGATCHI, GRADE 5

I guess I can admit this now. I was the one who called in the tip to the police hotline, and I leaked the item to the school paper. This is what I told them, and it was the truth. I had given it a lot of thought. It may not have been morally wrong for me to use Belch for *my* homework, but it was probably morally wrong for Snik and Kelsey, because they were using it as a crutch.

It *was* morally wrong for me to break the agreement we had made. But it would also have been morally wrong for me *not* to break it and let them continue using Belch. It was a lose-lose situation. In the long run, it would be better for Snik and Kelsey to do their own homework. But I didn't have the courage to confront them directly. In that regard, I am a coward.

SAM DAWKINS, GRADE 5

I couldn't believe it. How could he do that to us?

JUDY DOUGLAS, GRADE 5

I thought I was going to pass out. My life was over.

KELSEY DONNELLY, GRADE 5

I thought Snik and Judy were going to kill him! They were so mad. I told them they were being stupid. What was done was done. Brenton made the machine. He could do anything he wanted with it. It was our own fault. There was nothing we could do about it now. Even if Brenton hadn't told anyone, somebody would have found out eventually. I threw my arm around him and told him I forgive him.

SAM DAWKINS, GRADE 5

We had a lot of angry words, but what was done was done. We had to decide what to do next. Should we turn ourselves in? Run away from home? For the time being, we decided to stop using Belch and hope the whole thing blew over.

KELSEY DONNELLY, GRADE 5

I called Judy that night. I had to say something else that had been on my mind for a long time, and it was so obvious it was ridiculous. I told her that she liked Brenton and Brenton liked her. They might as well come out in the open about it.

Well, she denied it, of course. She said I was crazy. I didn't care. I knew I was right. I may not know much about math or geography, but I know when two people like each other. Brenton and Judy were going out with each other, and they didn't even know it.

JUDY DOUGLAS, GRADE 5

Well, I told Kelsey she was nuts about me and Brenton. But I will say this. Kelsey really impressed me. I was proud of her taking over like that, and I was glad we had the meeting. It made me feel a little better the next day in school.

But then Miss Rasmussen handed me a note that said Brenton, Snik, Kelsey, and I were "invited" to a meeting in Principal Wilson's office the next week. *Invited.*

This was it. We were going to be suspended. Kicked out of school. My life was over.

SAM DAWKINS, GRADE 5

So Judy says we should just admit everything and tell the truth about Belch. She says that when criminals plead guilty to a crime, they get a lighter punishment than if they claim they're innocent. I tell her she's crazy. She'll never get into law school someday if they ever find out she cheated her way through fifth grade. She's upset, of course. She says she never wanted to use a machine to do her homework in the first place.

Then Brenton says it might be possible to destroy any evidence that Belch ever existed. He could erase all our data and wipe the hard drive clean.

Now *that* sounded like a good idea to me. We were in agreement. We decided to go into Principal Wilson's office the next week and deny everything. We'd pretend there was never any such thing as a homework machine.

Chapter 9

May

SAM DAWKINS, GRADE 5

So the four of us gather at my house that Saturday. We didn't all have to be there just to erase all the data. I guess we wanted to say good-bye to Belch. After all, it had been an amazing machine, at least before everything went wrong. It deserved a decent good-bye.

Brenton sits down at the keyboard and starts doing his thing. He says it would only take a few minutes to destroy all the data and erase the hard drive. But five minutes go by and he's still fooling with it. He has this worried look on his face.

BRENTON DAMAGATCHI, GRADE 5

Something was wrong. I had never locked the files or password protected them, but something

125

was preventing me from deleting them. I tried everything.

KELSEY DONNELLY, GRADE 5

Judy started to panic. She was grabbing Brenton by the shoulders and asking, "What's the matter? What's the matter?" He told her to stop it because he couldn't concentrate. He kept wiping the sweat off his forehead. The machine wasn't letting him delete anything.

JUDY DOUGLAS, GRADE 5

Finally, I couldn't take it anymore. I grabbed the power cord and just yanked the plug out of the wall.

KELSEY DONNELLY, GRADE 5

Judy went nuts and pulled the plug. We all thought that would be the end of it. But nothing happened! Belch was still on the screen and the little red power light didn't go out. Then she *really* went nuts.

BRENTON DAMAGATCHI, GRADE 5

Apparently, in the months we had been using the machine, it somehow discovered a way to conserve its energy or run without a traditional source of electricity. That's how intelligent it was. It had probably discovered some obscure Web site that described an alternative energy source that we couldn't begin to understand. I was frustrated that I could not seem to turn the thing off, but at the same time I marveled at the power of artificial intelligence. I was proud of it, in a way. It had evolved, with no help from me.

SAM DAWKINS. GRADE 5

It was like some weird science-fiction movie where the scientist creates this machine that becomes too powerful and develops a mind of its own and gets out of control and turns evil and tries to take over the world! I told Brenton to stop kidding around and just turn the thing off, but he couldn't. It was too smart. Judy was out of her mind. We all were.

JUDY DOUGLAS. GRADE 5

The machine was using *us* instead of us using *it*. We couldn't stop it! There was no telling what it might decide to do. Brenton said it might be a good idea for us to go into another room to talk about what to do next. I asked him why, and he said, "Belch might be listening." That *really* freaked me out.

KELSEY DONNELLY, GRADE 5

There was no getting around it. We knew what we had to do. We had to destroy Belch. Not deprogram it or erase it or delete some stupid files. We had to destroy the thing, before it destroyed us.

SAM DAWKINS, GRADE 5

If there's one thing I'm good at, it's busting stuff. I have a few baseball bats in the garage. We could have just taken Belch outside and whaled on the thing and busted it up good. But the others said that the police or the FBI or whoever was snooping around asking questions would find all the little pieces all over my yard.

KELSEY DONNELLY, GRADE 5

We talked about all the ways we could destroy Belch. Judy suggested we take it apart piece by piece and then mail each piece to a different country. But we didn't have time for that. Snik wanted to set it on fire or stuff it full of firecrackers and blow it to smithereens. I said we should just open up the back and pour Cheez Whiz all over the insides. My mom once dropped Cheez Whiz on a calculator by accident and it never worked again.

JUDY DOUGLAS. GRADE 5

I just wanted it to go away, forever. They were throwing out all kinds of crazy ideas. We could melt it. Run it over with a bulldozer. Dig a hole in the ground and bury it so deeply, they wouldn't find it for a hundred years.

I guess I was the one who suggested we throw it into the Grand Canyon. I wasn't serious. It was just a dumb idea.

SAM DAWKINS. GRADE 5

Judy had a brilliant idea! We didn't even have to dig a hole. We live right next to the biggest hole in the world! It's like a mile deep. The Colorado River is at the bottom and it's almost three hundred miles long. The river would carry Belch away and we'd never see it again. It was foolproof.

JUDY DOUGLAS. GRADE 5

Why would I be part of such a crazy plan? I don't know. Sometimes, when I'm under stress, I don't think straight. Desperate people do stupid things. I didn't use good judgment. My brain wasn't working. Everybody thought it was such a great idea. I got swept up in it.

BRENTON DAMAGATCHI, GRADE 5

It was like chess. We were in Zugzwang. Any move we made would have made our position worse. It seemed like our best and only option was to throw Belch into the Grand Canyon.

The bottom of the canyon is a mile down, but it's not a steep cliff like one of those Roadrunner cartoons. We couldn't just drop Belch over the edge and expect it to reach the bottom. It would be necessary to throw it a good distance to clear the rocks and trees. There was only one way to do that.

SAM DAWKINS, GRADE 5

The catapult! I thought, what a genius Brenton is! We'd get the catapult he built for school and bring it out to the South Rim of the canyon. We'd load Belch up into it and chuck the thing out of our lives forever.

KELSEY DONNELLY, GRADE 5

We waited until it was dark that night. The moon was full, I remember.

JUDY DOUGLAS, GRADE 5

We snuck into Brenton's garage and took out his catapult.

BRENTON DAMAGATCHI, GRADE 5

We took the catapult over to Snik's house and disconnected Belch. The red light never turned off.

SAM DAWKINS, GRADE 5

We loaded Belch onto the catapult.

KELSEY DONNELLY, GRADE 5

We wheeled the catapult over to the edge of the South Rim.

BRENTON DAMAGATCHI, GRADE 5

We found an isolated spot where it looked like it would be the shortest distance to the middle of the canyon.

KELSEY DONNELLY, GRADE 5

We made sure nobody was around.

JUDY DOUGLAS, GRADE 5

We all said good-bye. It was like taking an old

friend to the airport when they're moving away and you know you'll never see them again.

SAM DAWKINS, GRADE 5

We did a countdown. Ten . . . nine . . . eight . . . you know.

KELSEY DONNELLY, GRADE 5

Brenton pushed the button.

SAM DAWKINS, GRADE 5

And the thing just *flew*. You should have seen it. It crossed right in front of the moon. It was beautiful.

KELSEY DONNELLY, GRADE 5

We waited and waited. We never heard a splash or a crash. It was so far down. It was like the thing just vanished.

JUDY DOUGLAS, GRADE 5

I felt like a weight had been lifted off my shoulders.

KELSEY DONNELLY, GRADE 5

It was gone. It was over.

Chapter 10

Summer

SAM DAWKINS, GRADE 5

So school ends and we figure that's that. We got away with it. When we went into the principal's office for that meeting, we all played dumb. Homework machine? What homework machine? We pretended we didn't know what he was talking about. There was no evidence. Nobody could prove anything.

SAM'S MOM

I was dusting his room and I noticed that nice new computer wasn't there anymore. So I asked Sam where it was. He said Brenton asked for it back. I never called to check to see if that was true.

POLICE CHIEF REBECCA FISH

In early June, two backpackers came across some junk scattered around the bottom of the canyon, not far from the river. It had obviously been dropped off the rim. Luckily, the stuff didn't land on them. The backpackers alerted the park ranger. He contacted me.

Most of the pieces were too small to identify, but a few things looked like they might've been part of a computer. Who chucks a computer into the Grand Canyon? I put out the word to all the companies, organizations, and schools within ten miles. We have strict rules against dumping debris in a national park, you know. Visitors want to see nature, not somebody's trash.

MISS RASMUSSEN, FIFTH-GRADE TEACHER

I was washing the dinner dishes when our principal, Mr. Wilson, called and told me about pieces of a computer being found in the canyon. I didn't want to think that my students had anything to do with it. But I couldn't help but wonder. I told him I had a theory about what happened. I guess he made a few phone calls.

JUDY DOUGLAS. GRADE 5

That was probably the most humiliating experience of my life. School had just let out for the summer, and the four of us were called into the sheriff's office. We didn't know why. Our parents had to come, and Miss Rasmussen was there, too.

They sat us down at this big table, and in the middle of the table was a piece of Belch—the busted up keyboard. Nobody had to say a word. We knew what had happened.

SAM DAWKINS. GRADE 5

So they ask if anybody has anything to say, and we all just sit there not looking at each other. We could have blamed the whole thing on Brenton. I have to admit the thought crossed my mind. He invented the thing, right? And he couldn't keep the secret. He invented the catapult, too. But I couldn't rat him out. Brenton was my friend.

They had no evidence to tie us to the keyboard. It could have been anybody's keyboard. We could have gotten away with it. But then Judy just burst into tears and the jig was up.

KELSEY DONNELLY, GRADE 5

Judy started crying. So I got up and said, "It was all my fault. I did it."

Look, Brenton and Judy are geniuses. They shouldn't be prevented from going to college or doing something great with their lives because they made one stupid mistake in fifth grade. I didn't want Snik to take the rap either, after his dad died just a few months ago.

MISS RASMUSSEN, FIFTH-GRADE TEACHER

After Kelsey confessed, Judy shouted out that Kelsey was lying and that *she* was responsible for the whole thing. Everybody was shocked. I couldn't imagine Judy doing something like that. Then Brenton started yelling, "No! No! It was all MY idea!" The four of them started arguing about which one of them was most to blame, and instead of blaming each other, they all blamed themselves. They were all apologizing at once. I had never seen anything like it.

Thinking it over, I decided somebody else was really to blame. *Me.* I should have known what was going on months earlier. I was naive. I should have been more on top of things. They did it right under my nose. I so wanted my students to be successful, and I wanted to think they were successful because of my teaching. I guess the sad truth is that I still have a lot to learn about teaching, and I can't be so trusting with students in the future. I'll be more careful next year.

I told the kids that they didn't have to go off and invent a homework machine, because a homework machine already exists. It's called your brain.

POLICE CHIEF REBECCA FISH

When the kids were called into my office, that threw a scare into them. They confessed to everything. They seemed genuinely sorry for what they did, so I went easy on them. Made 'em hike down to the bottom of the canyon on a hot day and clean up the mess. Took 'em all day. Then I made 'em come in to the office over the summer and say what happened so we got it on record. Far as I'm concerned, this case is closed.

KELSEY DONNELLY, GRADE 5

I figured that was the end of it. School was over. Summer was here. I wouldn't be seeing Snik or Judy or Brenton again until September.

I don't know why, but I dyed my hair brown again and took out the belly button ring. I guess I just thought it was stupid.

JUDY DOUGLAS, GRADE 5

We were leaving the sheriff's office, and I knew that if I didn't say anything, I wouldn't see any of them for three months. So I worked up the courage and walked up to Brenton and asked him if he wanted to go out with me.

"What would that entail?" That's the way he put it. What would that entail? He cracks me up. So I told him it meant we might get together over the summer, you know, get some ice cream or pizza or hang out and talk and stuff. He said that sounded good to him. So I guess we're going out. I think so, anyway.

BRENTON DAMAGATCHI, GRADE 5

In honor of the beginning of summer, I decided to part my hair on the opposite side of my head. I really don't care about the way I look, but I read on some Web site that when you flush a toilet in the Southern Hemisphere, the water swirls clockwise, and when you flush a toilet in the Northern Hemisphere, the water swirls counterclockwise. So I thought it would be interesting to part my hair in opposite directions during summer and winter months. And Judy likes it better this way, too.

SAM DAWKINS, GRADE 5

I was thinking it over. In the beginning of the year, we all thought Brenton was a dork of the highest order. But I decided that Brenton was probably the coolest kid I ever met. And that includes me. Coolness doesn't come from having cool stuff or hanging with cool people. It's not cool to *try* to be cool. It's cool to *not* try to be cool. Brenton just does his own thing. He's one of these guys who is so uncool that he's cool. You know what I mean? You reach a point where you cross the line into coolness.

Anyway, after school ended I decided to call him up. He said, "To do what? We don't have any homework," and I said, "I don't know, you wanna play a game of chess?" and he said okay.

KELSEY DONNELLY, GRADE 5

I never thought I'd hear from Judy, but she called me up right after school ended. She said that Brenton and Snik were going to play chess over at Brenton's house and she was going too and did I want to come? Brenton's parents weren't home, but my mom said it was okay so I said sure.

By the time I got there, Snik and Brenton were already going at it hot and heavy. All year long, Snik refused to play Brenton and now they were finally playing each other. I mean, it was intense in there. It was like the Super Bowl of chess. The two of them were staring at the board so hard, I thought it was going to burst into flames. I didn't say a word.

All I knew about chess was what Miss Rasmussen told us. I counted up the pieces on both sides and Brenton had one more pawn than Snik. That was the only difference. So I knew it was a close game.

Every so often, Brenton would mutter something mysterious like, "classic Sicilian defense" or "Hmm, the old Benko Gambit." I had no idea what he was talking about. I'm not sure if Snik did, either.

JUDY DOUGLAS, GRADE 5

Brenton was sweating and fidgeting and talking to himself. I couldn't believe Snik was giving him a good game. I remember thinking back in

September how Snik was so dumb. And now he was holding his own at chess with the smartest guy in maybe the whole world. I was rooting for Brenton, of course, because he was my boyfriend.

KELSEY DONNELLY, GRADE 5

We took a break to eat some cookies Mrs. Damagatchi had left and I noticed that Brenton and Judy were holding hands. Holding hands! So I say are you two going out or what? Brenton just looked all embarrassed, but Judy said yeah we're going out. I knew it!

So while they were off being all lovey-dovey with each other, Snik came over to me and asks me if I want to go get ice cream or something after the game. Can you believe that? Sam Dawkins actually asked me out!

I tried to be cool about it. I said, "Are you just asking me out because Brenton and Judy are going out, or do you really want to go out with me?" And he says, "I really want to go out with you. I wanted to ask you out ever since school started, but I was too shy."

Him, shy? Unbelievable! I couldn't resist giving Snik a hard time. I said, "You need Brenton Damagatchi to give you the courage to ask a girl out? How pathetic!" Then I said sure I'd go out with him.

BRENTON DAMAGATCHI, GRADE 5

It reminded me of the classic Karpov-Korchnoi game in 1978. I tried a queenside advance, but Snik had two aligned bishops clogging up the middle of the board. I offered him a poisoned pawn, but he was too smart to fall into that trap. Snik doesn't make dumb mistakes the way he used to.

He was a much stronger player than he had been a few months earlier. I was up one piece, but he had the stronger position. I kept looking at the board, trying to come up with something that would trip him up.

It was hopeless. Finally I tipped my king over and we shook hands. He had beaten me.

SAM DAWKINS, GRADE 5

I tried to be cool about it, but it was impossible. My heart was jumping out of my chest. I had just beaten Brenton Damagatchi, the kid who was so smart that he got every kid in America to wear red socks to school! If I can beat him, that must mean I'm pretty smart, too.

JUDY DOUGLAS, GRADE 5

So Snik beat Brenton and I thought nothing could beat that. But suddenly the doorbell rang. Brenton asked me to see who it was. I opened the door and there was a guy in a suit standing there. He looked familiar to me, but I couldn't place the face. Then he sticks out his hand and says his name is Richard Milner.

KELSEY DONNELLY, GRADE 5

Judy let out this scream from the front hallway. We heard the door slam and we all came running over. She was hysterical. She said it was the guy she saw on the street. I asked her what his name was and she said it was Milner. Milner! That was the guy who was stalking me online! He was right outside the door! I freaked out.

SAM DAWKINS, GRADE 5

Kelsey starts in screaming, "Call the police! Call 911!" I didn't know what to do. Judy and Kelsey were screaming and crying and running around like an asteroid was about to hit the house. They said the guy was with the FBI or the CIA and we would all be going to jail. I looked around for a baseball bat or something I could hit the guy with if he tried to break down the door.

BRENTON DAMAGATCHI, GRADE 5

I opened the door. What else could I do? The man was just standing there.

SAM DAWKINS, GRADE 5

So Brenton opens the door and asks the guy if he's with the FBI. He says no. Brenton asks him if he's with the CIA. He says no. I can't take it anymore so I ask the guy who he is and what he wants from us. He says nobody's in trouble and we didn't do anything wrong. That calmed the girls down a little.

JUDY DOUGLAS, GRADE 5

The guy showed us his business card. He says he's in the marketing business and he works for a company that sells stuff to kids. I asked him why he was stalking us and he said he wasn't stalking us. He simply wanted to talk to us.

SAM DAWKINS, GRADE 5

I asked the guy what kind of stuff he sells to kids. He says everything. Breakfast cereal. Toys.

Toothpaste. Clothes. Video games. Music. So I ask what does that have to do with us?

KELSEY DONNELLY, GRADE 5

The guy says he's been looking for kids who influence other kids. You know, like, kids who are the first to do stuff and then everybody else starts doing the same stuff. Kids who start trends. He's been trying to talk to us for a long time, he said, because he thought red socks day and inside-out day were brilliant and effective marketing plans. If Brenton could get every kid in America to wear red socks to school, he said, imagine how much breakfast cereal his clients could sell. Imagine how many toys, clothes, tubes of toothpaste, video games, and CDs his clients could sell. He said he would pay Brenton if he would help him.

SAM DAWKINS, GRADE 5

I'm thinking, how much? I mean, this could be bigger than McHomework!

JUDY DOUGLAS, GRADE 5

Basically, the guy wanted Brenton to help him trick kids. He wanted Brenton to spread the word that certain products were cool, so his clients could make more money. I didn't think it was very nice and I told him so. I told him that kids don't need anyone to tell them what to buy. Most toys are junk anyway. We can make up our own minds about which video games to play and CDs we should listen to. We can make up our own minds about what's cool.

But of course, it was Brenton's call. He invented the machine. He was the computer genius.

BRENTON DAMAGATCHI, GRADE 5

I thought it over. I told the guy I'd like to go into business with him. Judy was really mad. Then I told the guy I didn't want to sell toothpaste and I didn't want to sell clothes or CDs or video games. He says, "Well, what do you want to sell?" I told him I don't want to sell some product to the kids of the world. I want to sell an *idea*. A really good idea that I'd been working on in my head. The guy was all excited. He asks, "What's the idea? What's the idea?" I looked around like it was a big secret that I didn't want anyone else to hear. Then I whispered it in his ear: "Do your homework."

The guy left. I don't think he'll be bothering us anymore.

The animals were the first to realize something was wrong. They always are. At 3:48 p.m. that Tuesday afternoon, the birds in Cape Bluff suddenly stopped singing. Cows huddled close together in the field. Dogs began running around erratically.

Animals have a sixth sense about these things. Maybe it's infrasound—low frequency rumbles that are below the threshold of human hearing.

Anyway, the animals knew before the people. They just knew.

To anyone's eyes in Cape Bluff, at first it looked like a whopper of a thunderstorm was approaching. The cumuliform clouds that dotted the sky all morning had, without anyone noticing, joined into one gigantic darker cloud mass covering the sky and blocking out the sun.

But there was something different this day. The sky took on a sickly yellow/greenish hue. At the local weather station a few miles down the road, a meteorologist jotted down the time in his logbook.

The rains came down for a while, not too heavy. There was even some hail. Then there was an eerie quiet.

Richard Ackoon, the young rapper sitting on his porch, looked up. There had been a sudden change in pressure. The air felt heavy, and hot, like it was too close to his face. He found it hard to breathe.

The enormous cloud was moving fast, and then, suddenly, the wind stopped. It was peaceful. The leaves in the trees tilted up gently, as if they were looking at the sky.

No funnel cloud was visible. Not yet. There was a subtle swirling mist, but nobody could see it. The tube of air was horizontal at first, but gradually the rising air pushed it vertically, until it resembled a spinning top.

Elke Villa, the girl who had been singing in the shower, suddenly stopped when she heard a tornado siren go off in the distance.

Cape Bluff is in the heart of Tornado Alley, a vast area that stretches from parts of Texas to Minnesota. Everyone who lives within that region knows what to do when the tornado siren blares. In school they had tornado drills once a month.

Elke quickly rinsed off and got out of the shower. She threw on a T-shirt and shorts, went into her bedroom, and pulled the mattress off her bed. Then she dragged it into the bathroom. She picked up her dog, Lucky, climbed into the tub, and pulled the mattress over the two of them. She and Lucky would stay there in the bathtub until the all-clear signal sounded.

Mrs. Mary Marotta quickly screwed the cap on the Marshmallow Fluff jar and grabbed the remote control to her TV. She flipped away from *Oprah* and turned to The Weather Channel. The screen was flashing TORNADO WARNING FOR FOUR STATE AREA. But almost instantly the power in her house went out and the screen faded to black. She rushed to get a flashlight and transistor radio from her pantry.

"Mommy, the TV went off!" cried her daughter, Elsie, from the living room. Elsie was in second grade, and her little brother, Edward, was in first.

Mrs. Marotta grabbed each of them by the arm, and hustled them outside to the prefab bomb shelter constructed belowground in the backyard. It had been built in the 1950s, in case of a Russian atomic blast.

When he heard the siren, Paul Crichton, the young guitar god, grabbed his most precious possession—his Strat—and crawled under the workbench in the corner of the basement. That's what his parents had taught him to do. If anything was going to fall on him—like the entire house—he would be protected.

At The Fontaneau Ballet Studio, Julia Maguire and the other students were hustled away from all that glass—the picture window in the front and the giant mirror that covered one whole wall of the studio. The school had no basement. The students were led—in an orderly fashion—into the office and instructed to crouch down in the corner to make as small a target as possible. The leotard-clad girls covered their heads with notebooks, backpacks, or in some cases, just their hands.

All over Cape Bluff, people rushed to prepare for a disaster. Some were hiding in closets, hoping to put as many walls as they could between themselves and the wind. People huddled on the floors of interior rooms, avoiding halls that opened to the outside in any direction. Kids rushed to put on their bike helmets, batting helmets, and hockey masks. Anything to protect themselves from flying objects. Some people crawled into metal trash cans. Parents were exchanging final glances, just in case they would not see one another again.

The storm picked up momentum as it rushed through town. People who were unfortunate enough to be out on the streets of Cape Bluff watched the black funnel approaching, fully aware that a falling tree, power line, or lightning bolt was just as dangerous as the tornado itself.

The smart ones jumped in a nearby ditch and lay there. That's the safest place outdoors, unless of course, you get swept away by a flash flood.

All over town, a continuous rumble could be heard in the distance. As the funnel moved closer, it became a muffled *whoosh*ing sound, like a waterfall or air rushing past an open car window driven at high speed. The roar grew sharper and louder, until it sounded like a freight train or jet engine.

It was officially an F4 tornado. The wind speed topped out at 260 miles per hour. But nobody knew the speed for sure, because at the weather station the device they used to measure wind speed blew away. Trees began to bend, and finally snap.

Some people—some foolish people—ran around their houses frantically opening the windows. They had been told that if the windows are open, it allows a tornado to pass through more easily and cause less destruction.

They were wrong.

The black funnel, now visible for miles, began to stab the earth like a dagger from the clouds. The snakelike tail flipped back and forth underneath it, licking one neighborhood for a minute or two before dancing on to the next one, like a bee trying to decide which flower to pollinate. It lashed out as if it had a purpose, an insatiable twisted mind intent on destroying anything below.

Like a carousel out of control, debris was swirling overhead. Bricks, beams, concrete, chairs, tables, clothes, toys, jewelry, and family heirlooms. Kitchen knives were flung 150 feet per second, impaling anything in their path. Years later, one would be found at a construction site, eight feet below the ground.

At Pete's Lumber Company on the north side of town, two-by-fours were being tossed around like Popsicle sticks. A hundred-year-old oak tree was yanked out by the roots. Cars were flying through the air like Frisbees.

At Cape Bluff Elementary School, the door to the library was ripped off its hinges. Water flooded inside, and virtually every book in the library was ruined.

At Booker's Stamps and Coins, the entire inventory was swept away. In an instant, a lifetime of work that had been so carefully collected and stored was gone.

Objects were plucked off the ground and thrown every which way. A pair of German shepherds was picked up and carried a quarter mile from their home. Miraculously, neither was hurt. An entire maple tree would be found, intact, two miles from where it grew. Forty miles away, a phone bill from a Cape Bluff resident would be found on the street. Debris would be picked up as far as eighty miles away.

Don Potash, the young comedian, had been home alone, watching his portable battery-powered DVD player. He had headphones on and hadn't heard a thing. As he listened to Jerry Seinfeld tell jokes about doing laundry, Don's house began to shudder as if a giant was shaking it. The building vibrated as the roar grew steadily louder. Don was concentrating heavily as he copied down the jokes in his special notebook that was filled with his favorite comedy routines.

By the time Don realized anything was going on, the aluminum siding was being ripped away from the frame of his house like a banana peel. And then, the building literally *exploded* and flew away. Seconds later, you couldn't even tell that a house had ever been on that spot. It had been wiped clean.

All that was left was Don Potash, sitting where his house used to be, dazed and confused, with the headphones still on his head.

And then, after all that . . . nothing. The tornado had done the only thing it knew how to do—destroy things indiscriminately. It suddenly dissipated, exhausted, like a car that had run out of gas.

Just ten minutes after the tornado started, it was all over.